*For Elaine Murphy
and Lucinda Williams*

*With special thanks to my editor, Alison Berry,
and to Mr Horsler of Icknield High School
for lighting the spark*

23 *Tudor Avenue*
Benbridge
Trowton TR0 9AF

Ms Alexa Deerheart   16 January
THE BIZZ

Dear Alexa

Oh, God! I think I'm going to die. I'm sorry if this sounds dramatic but I feel as if I've been struck by lightning, hit by a thunderbolt, knocked down by a feather, dropped from the clouds . . .

This morning everything started normally. At 8 o'clock I was brutally awoken from a rather pleasant dream by my mother gently ripping the curtains apart with no more apology than, 'Move yourself, you great lump!' Lethal white light flooded the room as the bed-clothes were ruthlessly torn from my pale interesting body leaving me exposed like a vampire under a sunlamp.

I dressed casually: Dr Martens, ankle socks, school skirt and my sister's neon pink Spandex vest which I successfully concealed under two sweatshirts topped with my blue (chest 30!) V neck. Then, just to be ultra safe, I wrapped Auntie Paula's Dr Who scarf (circa 1976) three times round my neck and stuffed the ends into my blazer sleeves. A bit bulky but, quite

1

frankly, Rosalee can sniff out a borrowed sock at a distance of 50 metres – and that's on a bad day!

As soon as I sat down to breakfast, I felt nervous. Trying to look cool and relaxed is difficult for me at the best of times but wearing three sweatshirts makes you feel downright shifty. I can tell you. At first nobody noticed anything. Rosalee had her head stuck inside *True Love* and Mum was busy making my toast and Marmite. Mum had just put my breakfast on the table, when she stood back for a second and said, 'For goodness' sake, Gilly, what on earth do you look like!'

'I think I've got a cold coming on,' I said rather cleverly. 'I thought I'd better wrap up.'

'But the heating's full on, it must be 100° in here, you silly girl,' she replied innocently. It was too late. Rosalee was sitting bolt upright, eyeballing me like I was the prime suspect in a murder case.

'What – have – you – got – on – under – there!' she screamed. 'Let's have a look.'

I resisted, of course, but in a second she'd gone for the throat and, after a brief period of near strangulation by Auntie Paula's scarf, the evidence was revealed.

'*She's wearing my pink Spandex!*' she yelled in a sort of agonized screech, more suitable for the discovery that your pet hamster had been used in a ritual murder. 'Get it off! Get it off!'

Everything went flying as she pulled me to

the floor, literally trying to tear the clothes from my back while Mum tried to tear her off me crying, 'For goodness' sake, girls!'

Well it all ended with me lying in a heap on the floor removing the sweatshirts one by one in humiliated silence with Rosalee standing over me like a triumphant Amazon and Mum sighing, 'Won't you girls ever learn to get on?' When I got down to the pink Spandex, Rosalee gave a snort. 'God, you look ridiculous in that – you haven't got any tits.' I tried to stand up but I slipped, landing smack in the middle of the decimated breakfast. When I finally got to my feet Rosalee made a noise like a horse in labour. She had just noticed the slice of toast and Marmite sticking to what would have been my left bosom, if I'd had one.

Well, Alexa, you may think that this is leading nowhere, but you'd be wrong. I think you need the background information to get to the heart of the problem that is eating away at me relentlessly and occupying my every waking thought. For it was on that morning that I first saw HIM. I'm nearly fourteen, and I was beginning to think there was something different about me. All of my friends seemed to be having love crushes of one kind or another, but me? Not a flicker. At first I thought it must be because I'm an ardent feminist (Chairperson of LSHYWAC – Langley Street High Young

Women's Action Committee) and unable to see men as little more than insectile. Then Judy Fry told me it was because I hadn't got any breasts yet, and without breasts you don't get 'stirrings' – whatever they are. But quite frankly I wasn't worried. Until now.

I walked to school, alone as usual. Not many from our class live near me. Luckily. For the fewer people who actually see my house, the better. It's a mock Tudor detached with CARRIAGE LAMPS and gives me a street cred of about minus zilch.

I met my best friend Annie outside the school gates. Annie is about four foot nothing, with a shock of ginger corkscrew curls. In other words she looks about nine years old, which is fine by me as when we're together I can imagine I'm an older sophisticated woman with long legs (when, in fact, I'm only five foot one myself). Anyway, Annie said, 'Hi, Gilly, good weekend?' 'Groovy,' I replied (referring to a visit from Grandma Freeborn who gave Rosalee and me five pounds each for 'being such good girls') and 'Not groovy,' (referring to the pink Spandex episode). I explained that I'd wanted to wear it to our LSHYWAC meeting to be held in the art room that evening. Annie and I are the founder members of LSHYWAC. We haven't had too much luck with recruits so far – just four of us from our class, including a girl called Phyllis Bean who's about as daft as a hedgehog in a brush factory

4

but who's always hanging round us and is useful for her grovelling, sycophantic tendencies.

Anyway, Annie and I took our places in the choir (which faces the main door) and had just launched into 'Oh, He so beautiful and divine' in our matchless sopranos when, behind the headmaster, in walked – a vision. At first I thought old Pennings had flipped and had invited a rock star to give us a talk (he sometimes turns up with what he calls a 'personality' to lecture us – usually some pathetic old fogey with nothing better to do than bore three hundred kids half to death). Then I noticed that the vision was wearing – a school uniform! Or part of it, anyway (as you've probably gathered, it's not compulsory in our progressive establishment).

Well, I swear that half the choir stopped singing and Judy Fry (usually a hundred per cent cool at all times) nearly broke her neck by turning it forty-five degrees south to watch his progress up the aisle. And then, Alexa, as he approached the choir he looked at me and smiled. OK, I could have imagined this. He could have been grimacing at the sight of Phyllis Bean who was standing next to me, dribbling as usual – I've been torturing myself with this self-doubt ever since – but whatever he was doing he was doing it in my direction. *I was in his line of vision.* What I'm trying to say is that he must have seen me and all that kept going through my head were those fateful words 'you've got no tits'. 'You've got no tits' was going round and round my brain like a curse in an echo chamber.

I cancelled our meeting that evening. His name is Jonathan O'Neil. He has dark curly hair that wisps around his ears. It shines. He's six feet tall (at least). He's got brown eyes and beautiful hands and I'm getting 'stirrings' all over the place – in my arms, in my legs, in my chest, in class, in the gym, in the cloakroom and here in bed while I'm writing this letter to you. Alexa, it's absolutely essential that I start growing breasts, and soon. Please help me.

Yours trustingly

Gilly Freeborn

23 *Tudor Avenue*
Benbridge
Trowton TR0 9AF

Ms Alexa Deerheart   24 January
THE BIZZ

Dear Alexa

Thanks a lot! You've really come through for me, haven't you? I must say that I find it absolutely thrilling that 'lots of girls go through life flat-chested and are perfectly happy'. Good for them! Let me tell you that this news has gone down like a lead balloon in this department. OK, thinking long term, I might save money on underwear, but who cares? You'd better think again. Things are getting desperate. Amazingly, Judy Fry has invited me to her party three weeks on Saturday. He'll be there!!! I need advice and I need it quick.

Looking forward to hearing from you *very soon*!

Yours in desperation

Gilly Freeborn

PS   Is it possible to be an ardent feminist and painfully in love at the same time? Annie says this is ideologically unsound and non-cool.

23 *Tudor Avenue*
Benbridge
Trowton TR0 9AF

Ms Alexa Deerheart   31 January
THE BIZZ

Dear Alexa

Thank you for your nice letter. I'm sorry if I sounded over the top but I felt depressed and desperate. I think that age fourteen was invented just to put kids through a load of agony to warn them that being grown up is going to be no big deal. The trouble is that you just don't *know.* You don't know anything. You don't know if your nose is suddenly going to receive an overdose of hormones and you'll wake up one morning with this enormous conk, like Uncle John's which looks like a potato with scarlet fever. You don't know if you're going to inherit Grandma Freeborn's hairy lip or even, dread of dreads, Auntie Paula's stubby legs and flat chest! There's this great inheritance of genes just waiting to spring itself on you. I once saw a photo of some great-grandma or someone who had this huge wobbly triple-tier chin. I hope to God I don't get *that*!

Thanks for the advice, but I'm afraid it's absolutely no use to me now, for I've discovered that I'm nothing more than a smudge on the face of humanity as far as Mr Jonathan O'Neil is concerned.

By Thursday morning our class had completely gone to pieces. After home ec, in which we spent an hour in the mind-expanding activity of making stuffed tomatoes, we had English with Mrs Goldstein. As it neared lunchtime she started asking what was the matter with us. It seemed impossible that she was blind to the tumultuous upheaval in our young lives. The whole class (with the exception of Phyllis Bean whose brain seems permanently tuned to a space in front of her eyes, and Tracey Mann who's too clever for such earthly concerns, and Annie who keeps giving me strange sideways looks) seems to have been VISION affected. Anyway, we're doing *Wuthering Heights* and just as Mrs Goldstein was telling us about the strange nature of Heathcliff's love for Cathy (we were, of course, all imagining ourselves in a windswept clinch with HIM on a wild Yorkshire moor) the bell rang.

We stampeded out like a herd of demented wildebeests to get the best place in the canteen. I sat at a table with Annie, Sarryan Crowhurst and Emily Clay. I had pathetically little on my plate and I wasn't eating what I had. My eyes were tuned on the door where HE would be making his entrance. Then I spotted Phyllis wending her way towards us wielding a mound of mashed potatoes with sausages sticking out all over like a load of unexploded bombs. Of course, she sat next to me.

'That's disgusting,' said Sarryan. 'My mum says sausages are made from . . . from PIGS' BALLS!' Oh, God. Poor Phyllis. Her mouth opened in a greasy 'O' and bits of prime pork banger dribbled from her lips in globs. Even I thought this was going a bit far. OK, Phyllis probably didn't know a pig's ball from a sow's ear, but that wasn't the point. You shouldn't torment the afflicted, should you?

Just at that moment, in walked THE VISION surrounded by what seemed like the whole of 11a. His blazer sleeves were pushed up; he had a tan and he was wearing TIGHT BLACK JEANS; his shirt was open at the neck. I felt as if I was having SPASMS inside. And of course I had to have Phyllis of the oozing sausage right next to me again. He probably thinks she's my best friend, or a blood relation at the very least. Next to Jonathan pranced Michael Barnes, who used to be a bit of a heart-throb, but who looked like a sort of mutant runner bean beside HIM.

Then in swept Judy Fry (carefully timed, I'm sure) like Scarlett O'Hara in *Gone with the Wind*. She looked at least seventeen, with her streaked blonde hair and wriggly hips. Even people in Year Ten looked like retarded adolescents in comparison. And cool as a fridge in a heatwave she floated past his table ever so slowly. The canteen went silent, except for THE VISION, who carried on talking, but he was watching her all the way to the counter where she said, 'Just a salad,' in this low sexy voice.

'God, look at that,' said Sarryan in undertones. And suddenly everything seemed hopeless.

I spent the afternoon in complete misery. Pennings was taking us for biology. He kept waffling on about protoplasm and membranes and vacuoles – just the kind of stuff we're going to need when we go out in the world. Imagine . . . 'Ms Freeborn, could you please explain the motivation behind your decision to join the board of the Equal Opportunities Commission?'

'Well, if you put a potato in a flat glass dish filled with water, shove in some sugar and wait for about three hours, the potato water turns pink and the result is that the potato is no bloody use to anyone.' I mean, really!

Anyway, I was staring down at my book, unseeing and unhearing. I was locked, vice-like, in this fantasy where Judy Fry was dancing with HIM at Manhattan Lights (a club I'm never allowed to go to, worse luck) when suddenly I drift in wearing a sleek black slash-skirt topped with Rosalee's neon pink Spandex and I've got bosoms and my legs have grown about ten inches; my hair has blonde streaks and is sort of wafting around my face in clouds. I've got this glow about me, a kind of aura. The music stops, he stops, everything stops. 'It's Gilly Freeborn!' people cry in mind-numbed astonishment. HE drops Judy's arm and just STARES at me, because I'm a vision. . . . Then Pennings' gravelly voice broke in like a foghorn in a symphony. 'Gillian Freeborn, could you please describe the difference between the nucleus and the protoplasm?'

'Well,' I said, drifting back into my polyester skirt and acrylic blue jumper, 'that is the question.'

'Of course it's the question, girl,' he snapped. 'And if you'd been paying attention instead of studying the back of your hand, you'd know the answer. The nucleus,' he continued, 'is the positively charged internal core of an atom around which others collect. Protoplasm is a colourless, jelly-like substance.'

Well, Alexa, I suppose that just about sums things up! Protoplasm by any other name is still protoplasm.

The bell rang, fortunately. Annie and I rushed to the home ec room to fetch out stuffed tomatoes (which now looked like billiard balls with dropsy) and made for the door.

On the way out, we saw them. She was leaning against the wall with her hands behind her back, sort of languishing, as if it were the most natural pose in the world. The worst thing was that HE was also leaning against the wall with his arm, facing her. The image is forever locked in my mind and keeps replaying itself like a video on overdrive. And Annie was going on and on about LSHYWAC and why did I keep cancelling meetings. But I wasn't listening, I couldn't hear. My face felt like a throbbing Belisha beacon and the closer we got the more I throbbed. And my knees started wobbling and my flesh started creeping.

Then just as we walked past, Judy said, 'Bye, *Gilly*.' Just like that. She did it on purpose. She knows. She *knows*. And just at that precise moment, with my name declared, my identity revealed, a stuffed tomato that had been eating its way through the paper bag, hurled itself out and went *splat*! on the concrete.

'Quick!' I hissed to Annie, and ran.

Annie caught up with me outside the sweet shop. We walked in agonizing silence for about three minutes. 'What's up?' she said. 'It was only a tomato, for heaven's sake.'

'Nothing is up,' I replied.

'Well, have I done something then?' she went on. Really, she is slow sometimes. Then it clicked.

'You don't fancy him, do you?'

'course not!'

'Then why've you gone all moody?'

'I'm not moody.'

'Why've you gone all funny, then?'

'I haven't gone *all funny*,' I snarled in a voice reserved almost exclusively for Rosalee.

We marched on in excruciating silence for another ten minutes, by which time I was thinking that this was the worst day of my life.

'I thought you hated men,' said Annie suddenly. 'I hope you're not going to go all soppy. What about LSHYWAC? You can't be a feminist and go all soppy over some, some . . . POSER!'

Well, Alexa, Annie's been my best friend practically for ever. After all, she probably wouldn't have even thought about being a feminist if it wasn't for me. But it seems this is something I'm going to have to live through by myself, like Isabella in *Wuthering Heights*.

What can be done? Is it all hopeless? Write soon and tell me the worst.

Yours

Gilly Freeborn

23 *Tudor Avenue*
Benbridge
Trowton TR0 9AF

Ms Alexa Deerheart   5 February
THE BIZZ

Dear Alexa

Yes, I understand that best friends are important. I understand that one day Jonathan O'Neil may be nothing more than a pinprick on the fabric of my memory (we're doing metaphors in English) while Annie could be my lifelong bosom friend and confidante. I understand that next week, next month, next year I may not give a stuffed tomato for Jonathan O'Neil. I understand that when I'm grown up, mature and sensible and probably doing some important world-changing job, this may all seem like the ravings of a demented adolescent. I understand all these things. But so what? Love has thrown its vice grip round my heart. My will is not my own.

Annie came round yesterday. Things were pretty strained between us, I can tell you. She just sat on my bed swinging her feet saying stuff like, 'This is a nice duvet cover' and 'I think it's raining'. And I was saying stuff like 'Rosalee's got this Saturday job at ZAP' and 'the clothes are really expensive, though' and

15

'I'm getting on quite well with *Wuthering Heights*' and other penetrating, earth-shattering observations.

Then Annie said that it was a shame about Phyllis and that we ought to try to be nicer to her, sort of draw her out – find her hidden qualities. And I said I wondered if her acne was catching and Annie said, 'What if it is? A little acne never hurt anyone, it's what's inside that counts.' (Which always makes me think of livers and kidneys and intestines and stuff – mine could be green with knobs on for all I care.) Then Annie said she supposed I was worried that 'lover boy' wouldn't fancy me with acne, which was the first really nasty thing she has said to me in the whole history of our best-friendship. I said not to be stupid and I didn't care if all my hair fell out and my teeth turned rot yellow because I wasn't the slightest bit interested in Jonathan O'Neil, which was, as you know, A GREAT BIG WHOPPING LIE. And it was the sort of lie that makes you feel really stupid because you know it and they know it and then they've really got you.

So Annie looked me straight in the eye and said she wasn't going to Judy's party and she supposed I wasn't going either since I wasn't the 'slightest bit interested in Jonathan O'Neil' and who wanted to prance around with a lot of nerds anyway? And I said I might just pop in because I wanted to see inside Judy's house and Annie saw right through *that* and said,

'Oh, *really*' and 'Mmmmm' and smiled this silly, superior smile out of the corner of her mouth. I got really fed up with her and angry – just because she's undersized and hasn't started developing the sensitivities of young adulthood, she wants to hold me back with her. So I said that Sarryan had asked me to go with her and Em and so I probably would, at which point Annie dug her heel into my pile of *Bizz* mags and knocked them over.

She left in a huff muttering something under her breath that sounded like 'seems like feminism is dead in this house'.

I spent the rest of the afternoon making posters saying 'Langley Street High Young Women's Action Committee Needs YOU. Join now and help to improve . . .' But it suddenly all seemed rather daft – five or six adolescent girls campaigning for more toilets and the chance to play rugby – I mean, who wants to play rugby anyway, just a lot of mindless scrambling round in the mud running after balls.

So I decided that I'd join something where I could be really radical; some organization that had power and influence, where I could tackle crucial issues, strike a blow for the young women of the new millennium. I went into Rosalee's room, borrowed some of her 'Check it out!' notepaper and wrote a letter to Radical Feminists asking if they could use a young,

17

motivated nearly-fourteen-year-old with vision and ideas. We'll see what Annie thinks of *that*!

Sunday afternoon. I'm actually feeling quite miserable, Alexa. I don't see how Annie and I can be proper friends again, and also she's got the miniature city we made together when we were eight and I don't suppose I'll ever get it back now, even though I did most of the work and it was my idea in the first place.

After lunch, Dad called me an old misery guts and said why didn't I take up the drums or the guitar and get into some music like he did at my age? And Mum said she didn't want the house shaking to its foundations and the neighbours complaining and why didn't he grow up? And Rosalee said I was just another self-obsessed, angst-ridden prepubescent and she wasn't surprised, especially as there was a great big boil erupting on my nose, which there wasn't. And I thought, Why don't you all shut up and go and drop dead somewhere, preferably in Outer Mongolia or Siberia and even that wouldn't be far enough.

I came up to my room, closed the curtains and have been sitting in deep and profound thought for about half an hour. Alexa, there's no need to reply to this. I have to think myself into a more positive frame of mind for Saturday week. I don't want to come across as a self-obsessed, angst-ridden prepubescent at the party, do I? In fact, that's the last thing I want.

Yours in gloom

Gilly Freeborn

23 Tudor Avenue
Benbridge
Trowton TR0 9AF

Ms Alexa Deerheart   11 February
THE BIZZ

Dear Alexa

Yesterday I received the following letter:

Dear Ms Freeborn
Thank you for your interest in our organization. We are of course always delighted to hear that there are motivated young people out there ready to take part in the struggle for true equality, the achievement of which, I fear, is still a long way off. However, because we are sometimes forced to take extremely radical action in the furtherence of our cause, it is necessary to restrict our membership to those over eighteen.

I am very sorry to have to turn you away. But I do hope that you will write to me again when you reach eighteen as we could certainly use as many forward-thinking young people as we can get. In the meantime, may I suggest that you use your energies locally? Perhaps you could start a group at your school. Get your classmates motivated. Campaign for equal opportunity on the sports field; lobby for the introduction of compulsory women's studies; fight for equal access to computer hardware – and make sure you girls are represented in numbers where the real decisions are made!

There is much valuable groundwork to be done by our idealistic young people.

Onwards the struggle!

Yours sincerely
Henrietta Boyce Philips
Membership Secretary

Such are the ironies of life! How bloody patronizing I say. Still, what I've decided is to make LSHYWAC more radical, get us moving on some really serious issues. I took the letter to school and read edited bits within earshot of Annie. 'Radical Feminists are right behind us,' I said to Sarryan. 'Why don't we set up a special committee to draw up some plans?'

Annie went pink around the ears and then stood up really slowly, giving me that new sideways smile, which she must have been cultivating because it's now turning into a sort of sneer.

Anyway, I'm going to arrange a big LSHYWAC meeting as soon as the party is out of the way and I've had time to get down to some serious thinking. I'm going to write a speech.

I am cheering up. Sarryan's going to lend me her skin-tight black hipsters for the party. About five of us from our class are going. And about five of us are hoping that Judy Fry is suddenly going to erupt in double acne with matching pus-filled warts on the night and we'll all come into our own. But no one could feel like I do. There's this great bubble of excitement in my stomach at the thought that I'll actually be in the same room as THE VISION. That I may even be able to *touch him*, accidentally of course; that he'll see me completely out of school uniform, looking pretty grown up and without Phyllis Bean attached to me doing something disgusting. It's even possible that he may *dance with me* – greater miracles have happened, like the feeding of the five thousand or the discovery of penicillin. He may even realize that Judy is nothing more than an empty shell of legs and hair.

There are all these possibilities and more, which brings me to the point of my letter. Is there *anything* I can do, Alexa, to appear sophisticated, older, taller, more attractive?

Yours

Gilly Freeborn

23 Tudor Avenue
Benbridge
Trowton TR0 9AF

Ms Alexa Deerheart   16 February
THE BIZZ

Dear Alexa

It's nearly Saturday. Mum's being OK about
the party, and so is Dad. Even Rosalee seems
to have a self-imposed amnesty on sarcasm –
she hasn't called me an underdeveloped
amoeba brain for at least three days (probably
due to her state of catalepsy brought on by the
materialization of Greg – some spotty
sportsbag of a boyfriend that nobody's been
allowed to meet). Maybe they've all just
realized that this is pretty important to me,
that's why I'm being fairly low key about it,
sort of cool.

Alexa, I'm in good spirits but I'm still left
with two problems; the first is that there is
absolutely zilch happening on the bosom front.
No growing pains, or even the hint of a growing
pain, which would be something. I've decided
to take your advice and wear something loose,
with things hanging down – a couple of scarves
should do the trick – but this just sort of
camouflages the problem, doesn't it? I mean,

pretty soon we're going to have to face things head-on unless developments get under way.

My second worry is that, although I've decided to take your advice about being 'patient, confident and relaxed and just waiting for things to happen' I don't really know what to do if they *do* start happening, if you know what I mean. You see, I've never really kissed anyone properly, incredible as it may seem for a nearly-fourteen-year-old. But as I said before, I just haven't had the urge, until now. So I was thinking that I might try to get some practice at the party, just a trial run with some nonentity to get the hang of it for when the big moment comes. Nothing more, though. I'm still trying to assimilate the facts of life into my psyche.

We didn't have sex education at our school. For some reason Langley Street High got left off the great list of those to be sexually enlightened. Judy Fry (advanced even in those days) told me about it in the home ec room when I was eleven. 'You mean you don't *know*!' she asked incredulously. And then she took great delight in divulging the gory facts in graphic detail. She even drew a diagram on the back of my toad-in-the-hole recipe. I must say that I was absolutely horrified. It seemed incredible that respectable human beings who had never harmed anyone were forced to submit themselves to this humiliating degradation just because they wanted to have children.

So I asked Mum that evening, thinking she would tell me not to listen to such filthy rubbish, that it was just the sort of smut you get from eleven-year-olds who don't know any better. But she just kept doing what she was doing, which was polishing the leaves of our Swiss cheese plant, and didn't even look up.

'Well, Gilly,' she finally said, '*Well*. . . .' and then she just admitted it – OUTRIGHT! However, such a brain-scrambling revelation wasn't to be taken lying down. I was thinking of Tiffany in 'EastEnders'. 'Well, if it's true, why do people who don't want babies do it then?' I had cried triumphantly, throwing a superior look at Rosalee.

'Well, w-ell,' said Mum, going red in the face and gulping. 'They do it because they like it.'

'LIKE IT!' I couldn't help myself, I screeched.

'God,' said Rosalee, 'are you naive!'

'But surely *the Queen* doesn't do it,' I went on, refusing to accept defeat.

Then to my horror Dad, who I hadn't realized had been sitting round the corner, burst out laughing, which I thought was a bit much. He nearly fell off the sofa at the thought of our monarch being subjected to this tortuous humiliation. And for some reason he picked me up and kissed me and said, 'Oh, Gilly, you're priceless!' while Rosalee looked at me as if she thought I were worth half a p at a push.

All this was beyond me and, quite frankly, it still is. But I've got a nasty feeling it's got something to do with these *spasms* I keep having. Still, I made up my mind then and there that I was *never* going to do it. And nothing's changed. I'm gonna go for artificial insinuation every time, I can tell you.

Yours

Gilly Freeborn

Ms Alexa Deerheart   19 February
THE BIZZ

Dear Alexa

Oh, joy of joys! I feel pretty speechless after last night. So I thought I'd better get it all down in words before I forget. Mum keeps calling me a 'great dream of a girl' and Rosalee keeps looking at me suspiciously and checking her wardrobe every five minutes, just in case the reason for my blissful state is the surreptitious requisition of some remnant or other. Dad doesn't seem to be saying much at all these days. He's been in a horrible mood and when he does open his mouth he says things like 'Oh, *God*' and 'bloody hell', which I think is a bit much with a sensitive young woman about.

Anyway, as you've probably guessed, it was the party yesterday. I spent the afternoon down town buying some sparkly eye gloss and a pair of silver dangly earrings, which were just the things to lift my level of sophistication to new heights. On the way home, I met Emily and we went for doughnuts in the Fresh Bake. We talked about what she was wearing and what I

27

was wearing and what Judy Fry would probably be wearing and who would be going and who would be getting off with who. And I thought, Annie's missing all this excitement, just because she's jealous and stubborn.

I spent an hour and a half getting ready. This is what I wore: sparkly eye gloss and mascara, silver dangly earrings and blusher. A new pair of knickers from Marks and Spencer, pink popsocks, Sarryan's skin-tight black hipsters, a very baggy blue T-shirt (new) and three silk scarves (two of Mum's and one with zebra stripes that Auntie Paula left behind on one of her flying visits). Then I brushed back my hair and sprinkled it all over with sparkly gel. The end result was quite striking – I mean, it was difficult to miss me unless you were a cross-eyed myopic wth conjunctivitis.

Sarryan arrived at eight. She was wearing: a funky black fluffy jacket over a skin-tight black halter dress with a hole in the back, black shiny tights and strappy black platform shoes. Sarryan's about the only one in our class with real genuine cool – her hair is jet black and spiky and she's got three earring holes in one ear. I think she looked fantastic, but I could see Mum thinking, what was she doing letting her precious little girl out with this femme fatale woman of the world. I know she doesn't like Sarryan, just because she lives in a flat in the Wellington Road, which is the stupidest reason for not liking anyone that I've ever heard.

Then Mum said what time should she pick us up and I said it was OK because Sarryan's brother was picking us up. And Mum said that was the first she had heard about Sarryan having a brother and Dad was coming and that was that.

And I said to tell him not to ring the bell *under any circumstances* and that we would wait three houses down to the left at precisely half-past twelve and that *even if we were a bit late* he was *to wait* because we would definitely be coming and even if he was *forced* to come to the door because the roof was on fire or the house was being invaded by a savage gang of sex-starved football hooligans he was to pretend to be a mini-cab driver, and *had she got that* because I was just about the only nearly-fourteen-year old in the world whose parents hadn't evolved with the times but had got stuck in a time warp about 1876.

To my surprise, Mum kissed me and said that I looked very nice. And when Rosalee came through the door carrying about twenty-five ZAP bags full of things she couldn't afford, Mum shot her a look as if to say, Don't you dare say anything; don't even try opening your mouth, for which I was grateful. I don't think I could have stood any of Rosalee's cryptic sartorial observations. I was strung up like a violin string on top C.

I couldn't see anything at first, except for a few blurred shapes in the hall. The music was really loud and sort of shot through your bones like a road drill. I got this great surge of something that felt like excitement and pure terror mixed together. HE was here. Somewhere in this seething mass his lovely body moved, freely accessible to the eye and more importantly to the touch – a brief, accidental brush of the shoulder was not entirely beyond the realms of reality.

Sarryan just stormed right into the kitchen as if she went to parties every night of her life (which she probably does) and knew exactly what to do. After a few agonizing minutes in which I examined every item in my bag with intense concentration, she reappeared carrying two paper cups of punch and strode purpose-fully into the living room with me clinging on to her like a leech with an insecurity complex. The first thing we saw was HIS glorious frame. I thought my heart would burst right out of my chest. He was wearing a soft, black leather jacket over a funky striped T-shirt and Levi 501s. The second thing we saw was this flash of red welded to his body; it was Judy Fry in a scarlet Lycra mini dress, dancing so close she looked as if she were attempting a human form of electro-magnetic fusion. Just as we had parked ourselves by the wall, Judy swirled round, causing her dead straight blonde hair to part and a big, blue eye stared right out at

30

me as if to say, You may as well dig a hole to Australia, Gilly Freeborn, and drop right through it.

The next minute, my worst fears were realized. Sarryan DISAPPEARED. One second she was standing next to me, the next she was dancing with Michael Barnes and I was left propping up the wall like poison ivy with greenfly. No one noticed me; no one even looked at me. I kept praying that someone I knew would float by, but of course they didn't. So I gulped down my punch and went in search of Emily, or anyone who looked vaguely familiar.

I found Em in the kitchen talking to a skinny boy in a leather jacket. I bounded up in a relaxed, confident sort of way and pulled at her sleeve. But all she said was, 'Oh, hi, Gilly,' and *turned round again* leaving me standing there like the Champion Dork of the World. No 'This is my friend Gilly' or 'Isn't this a great party' or 'You look nice' or *anything*. You'd never have guessed that we'd shared doughnuts and confidences in the Fresh Bake that very afternoon; you'd never have guessed that in a million years.

Everywhere people were kissing or dancing or talking and there was no way I could observe HIM in quiet obscurity. So I moved from room to room for about five minutes, pretending to look for someone, and all the time I was thinking, I've got another three hours of this, which means certain humiliation at the very least.

I killed half an hour queuing for the loo. Then do you know what I did? I went upstairs and hid myself under a pile of coats in the spare bedroom. Pathetic! Never had I felt more like a self-obsessed angst-ridden prepubescent in my life and I thought about all the excitement and getting ready and buying the dangly earrings and burst into tears right there and then under the coats of about fifty purposeful, confident, attractive people all having the time of their lives downstairs and not giving a wet toe rag for Gilly Freeborn.

After about an hour and a half in which I had thrown Sarry and Em out of LSHYWAC for 'behaviour unbecoming to the cause' and had reinstated Annie as 'the very best friend I had but didn't know it', the door opened. 'I think they're in here' said Sarryan's voice, her hand groping about dangerously close to my left ear. That's all I need, I thought in mortal terror. To be betrayed by an ear would be the crowning glory of an evening that ranked among the most cringeous of all time.

Escape by a finger's breadth. 'I wonder what's happened to Gilly,' Sarryan said, lighting up a fag. 'She seemed a bit nervous.'

'Yes,' said the traitorous Emily. 'Met her in town. She seemed overexcited. Trouble is she looks a bit young. Shouldn't think anyone'd fancy her.'

That did it! Although I felt about as attractive as a sick parrot with halitosis, I wasn't going to let *them* know it. As soon as the door closed I leapt out of my overcoat tomb, hitched up my hipsters, wiped off my runny mascara and examined my face in the mirror. 'You *do* look quite nice,' I told myself. 'You're really not bad looking AT ALL.' And there and then I decided I was going ahead with my trial kissing experiment. And like the princess in *The Frog Prince*, I was going to do it with the first thing I saw.

Wayne Cross! He wasn't that bad; he was leaning on the banister looking a bit lost and a bit short, but he was probably as good as anybody else still left after all the passable ones had paired off. And after seeming a bit taken aback by my sudden intense interest in his innermost thoughts about the party, life, the universe and everything, he grabbed me. There followed one of the most indescribably revolting experiences imaginable.

He pinned me against the wall and began *sucking* at my mouth, slurping and slobbering like a bloodhound with salivitis. I tried to move but his face was clamped to mine, vice-like, while rivers of spit ran down my chin to land in a pool in my neck. He made some funny grunting noises and began groping about in the labyrinth of my scarves. Ha! Tough luck, mate. You won't find anything *there*, I thought. Even if I had bosoms you'd be the last person

I'd let get their sweaty mitts on them. I think he must have been holding his breath because all of a sudden he stopped and gulped some air, obviously needing oxygen to fuel him up for another stint. I took the opportunity to turn my head aside but, would you believe it, he started *licking my ear out*. I thought, Really, your first kiss is supposed to be a poetic, poignant experience; nobody tells you you can be in danger of being forced to drink gallons of some creep's saliva.

I had just about had enough; enough of the party, enough of Sarryan and Emily, and enough of pretending to be relaxed and confident and 'waiting for things to happen'. I broke away from grunting Wayne, stumbled over the bodies on the stairs and went into the hall. Just as I was making my way to the kitchen the living room door opened and HE came out. He was behind me, but I sensed his presence; I sensed his strong brown arms and his long legs. The hall was bathed in soft light and he was pushing by me, touching me.

Then the most marvellous thing happened! I KNOCKED MYSELF OUT! I must have been dizzy from my session with Wayne for I tripped over Michael Barnes, who was lying on the floor in a clinch with Sarryan; I tripped over his foot and thwacked my head on the banister!

'Out of the way!' came HIS deep tones, drifting through my semiconscious state. 'I think she's concussed.' CONCUSSED! That word is now potent with the power of lyric poetry.

I felt myself being lifted up and even though I was coming round pretty fast, I stayed comatose, dropped my head on the side of his arm and affected what I hoped was a serene, angelic expression, the sort that drives men mad with tenderness. I sensed the lights being put on; I sensed people disentangling themselves and standing up. I heard Judy's voice saying, 'She's all right, she'll come round in a minute.' I could feel the hate waves emanating from her like red-hot lazers piercing my skin. But did I 'come round'? You can bet your life I didn't. Coming round was the last thing I was going to do. HE was holding me in his arms. OK, maybe not in the accepted sense of the phrase, but I'll tell you, spasms didn't come into it. I felt like a million-zillion butterflies were practising the Brandenburg Concertos over my body, all giving the performance of their lives. And I understood the meaning of BLISS and RAPTURE and SEVENTH HEAVEN all simultaneously and at the same time.

He laid me gently on the sofa and tenderly pushed the hair out of my eyes. Then somewhere in this orgy of bliss, I heard the doorbell ring, followed by 'minicab for Ms Freeborn' uttered in horribly familiar tones. Then came the word 'concussion' in HIS voice followed by 'Oh, dear God! Where is she? Has anyone called an ambulance?' and 'Who's responsible for this?' which I suppose seemed a bit of an overreaction from a minicab driver who wasn't supposed to know me from Adam.

I made a rapid recovery, sat up in a woozy sort of way and let my concerned parent help me out while HE explained what had happened. And at the doorway, Sarryan and Em came rushing up saying, 'You all right, Gilly?' and 'See you on Monday.' And I suddenly decided that they were all right and the world was all right; in fact everything was absolutely head-stunningly, mind-burstingly wonderful!

Well, to cut a riveting story short, after a dismal start the evening exceeded my wildest expectations. And after Mum and Dad had reassured themselves that I hadn't been blind drunk or drugged or sexually abused I was left to spend Sunday in a state of heavenly reflection, which not even Rosalee could spoil when she said I'd looked like an overweight Christmas tree fairy.

Well, Alexa, what do you think of that! Fate has dealt me an ace of hearts. Things could really be on the move.

Yours in ecstasy

Gilly Freeborn

Ms Alexa Deerheart   21 February
THE BIZZ

Dear Alexa

Oh, gloom of glooms! Have I made an indelible impression on the romantic sensibilities of Jonathan O'Neil? I shouldn't think so! No, not a bit of it. Monday morning assembly. I expected at least a concerned 'Hello' or a we-shared-a-special-moment look, but his head didn't swivel my way once. As I croaked out the harmony of 'Light up my anxious heart' my spirits sank right to the bottom of my battered old Doc Martens.

On the way to art, I hung back, giving him one last chance to acknowledge our special bond born from a simple twist of fate, but all I got was a brief glimpse of the back of his head as it disappeared into the bowels of the computer science department. Gone. It hardly seemed possible.

I'm planning to do art for GCSE. It's one of my best subjects, normally. But today I managed to spend an hour making 'Ellen Pugh with carnations' look like 'The Elephant Man with constipation'. Ellen wasn't very pleased, and neither was I. I think my academic life is being thwarted through my sufferings for love.

Morning break. There HE was, right in my path on the way to the canteen, talking to three nonentities in track suits. Oh, God in heaven! He was wearing *shorts*; his long brown legs went on and on and ended in sparkling white socks and black Adidas trainers. My heart gave a great lurch and I felt exactly as I had done when I was five years old and auditioning for the part of the good fairy in *Sleeping Beauty* – dumbstruck. For some reason, known only to qualified psychologists, my eyes just fixed on him. I couldn't help it. I was staring straight at him like a zombie with senile dementia.

'There's some funny girl staring at you,' said one of the track suits. On and on I went. Something was impelling me forward like a lemming on Judgement Day.

Finally, HE looked round. 'Oh. . . . Oh, hello. Didn't recognize you. You feeling all right now? No brain damage?'

'Uh-uh,' I replied in an I'm-completely-whacko sort of way which seemed to answer his question in the affirmative.

'Oh, good,' he said. 'Gotta go.' And I just stood there, frozen, watching his beautiful back disappear into the gym while another of the track suits said, 'God, there are some really weird chicks in this school.'

In the canteen I sat with Sarryan, Em and

Ellen, feeling about as low as a worm with skin disease.

'My God,' said Sarry, 'that was some stunt you pulled off at the party. You disappear for two hours and then reappear in the arms of the man himself. Judy was *furious* though she couldn't say anything.'

'Yeah,' I replied miserably. 'I was a real knockout.'

Alexa, the tide is at a low ebb; my ship has gone out. I'm going to throw all my frustrated energies into my essay on *Wuthering Heights*. Something's got to benefit from this tortured agony of thwarted desire.

Yours in rejection,

Gilly Freeborn

23 Tudor Avenue
Benbridge
Trowton TR0 9AF

Ms Alexa Deerheart   27 February
THE BIZZ

Dear Alexa

Half term. I wish Mum wouldn't keep calling me 'great lump' or 'great lazy lump'. I know she thinks it's a joke – she usually does it in the morning when, I admit, I'm sloth-like and sluggish and trying to fight the morning off – but it's getting on my nerves. After all, it's bad enough having to cope with a vertical chest without feeling that your own parents think you're a *lump*. And I'm really *not*, Alexa. Only I can't say anything, or they'll start teasing me, thinking that it's *ever so* funny that I've taken offence. And if Rosalee got hold of it there'd be no stopping her, she'll be calling me lump-head, and lump-brain and lump-nose.

And this is how I was feeling on Saturday, so I went round to Sarryan's to cheer myself up. I've always liked her house – it's like a different world. Annie and I live on *estates* – ghastly new estates of adolescent houses that haven't had any *experience* of life, if you know what I mean. Ours is the worst, Benbridge. Miles and miles of mock period houses, shining

40

and pristine, they really look daft. Benbridge is supposed to be 'the jewel of Trowton' – some clever dick came up with the madly original idea of a 'period' estate so up-and-coming yups could choose between a four-bedroomed 'Elizabethan' monstrosity or a detached 'Neo-Georgian' or 'Staggered Victorian Terrace'. We chose a three-bedroomed detached in Tudor Ave (would you believe) and moved in five years ago. I didn't mind it then – it was quite fun playing on the building sites – but now it just sucks at your soul because there's nothing here, *nothing*. Just miles and miles of flat boring streets that end in another estate that ends in a building site. There's a pub called the New Green Man, a shopping arcade with a mini-mart, an electrical goods shop, a cake shop and a florist. And that's it!

Sarryan lives on the other side of town, where they've still got some real houses left. They've got old bricks and nice windows and gardens with big trees in them. Sarryan's house is huge. She lives in a flat on the ground floor and her bedroom's got French windows that go out on to the garden. I took a blank cassette because Sarry said she'd copy her tape of the Contaminators for me as I 'ought to be getting into some bands' if I was going to cultivate my cool.

We were sitting on her bed with the music blaring

You're nothing but a worm, baby,
A wha-wha, wha-wha, wo-wo-wo-rm!

when Sarry suddenly said, 'What's up with you 'n' Annie then? Aren't you talking?'

'Hum, not really,' I said. It was rather difficult, Alexa, because on the one hand I wanted to say, 'She's a narrow-minded, physically retarded goody-goody and I hate her guts' but it seemed wrong, somehow, sort of betraying all the good things we had done. So I just said, 'Oh, it's just that we've outgrown each other. She's not interested in the same things.'

'Well, you can hang out with me and Em, if you like,' said Sarry. 'Only you'll have to learn a few things, like the switch.'

And she started teaching me this dance that she and Em have invented where you take two steps to the right, two steps to the left, then one backwards, then one forwards and then do this twiddly thing with your feet, all the time making jerky movements with your head. You do it to rapping music. Sarry put on the Eruptions' *Big Rap Talking Blues Number Nine* and cranked up the sound. The sun was pouring in and Sarry was laughing at me because I couldn't get the hang of it straight off and kept going right instead of left and left instead of right. Then we both did head jerks the wrong way at the same time and scrunched our skulls, which seemed so unbelievably funny that we collapsed on the bed in hysterics. And even though my head started throbbing, I didn't mind. I didn't feel like a big nothing lump any more.

On the way home, I imagined Sarry and me doing the switch on television. We'd developed it so it was really complex and sophisticated. It was hailed as the first new innovation in popular dance since break dancing, and Chris Evans was interviewing us on 'Music of the New Age'. I imagined HIM watching at home, suddenly sitting bolt upright, transfixed because he'd suddenly recognized the girl he had once saved from certain brain damage and never given a second thought. The camera zooms in for a close-up as I expound on the origins of the moves, the *meanings* of the gestures. My face is thin, my skin pale, my eyes big and blue and alive with creative intelligence. His heart feels fluttery. What has he thrown away? If only he'd waited just a few weeks, given her time to develop, this *swan* could have been his. He is full of soul-tearing regret at the wasted months with that bundle of brainless bones, Judy Fry. A tear drops from a lustrous lash. . . .

Yours

Gilly Freeborn

23 *Tudor Avenue*
Benbridge
Trowton TR0 9AF

Ms Alexa Deerheart   8 March
THE BIZZ

Dear Alexa

I've had a revelation! This is how it happened.
It was Wednesday afternoon and we were once
again ensconced in English lit.

'Emily Brontë was a tragic figure,' said Mrs
Goldstein.

'No, she wasn't.'

'I beg your pardon?'

'She wasn't tragic,' said Tracey Mann from
the back. 'She was misunderstood.'

'Well, yes, Tracey,' Mrs Goldstein went on.
'It's certainly true that she was misunderstood.'
Then she looked over the top of her glasses
and added, *'But she was tragic as well,'* in a
that's-enough-of-your-cleverdickery-Tracey-
Mann sort of voice. 'Now how many of you
know – '

'I'm sorry, Mrs Goldstein,' Tracey went on
in her you-may-be-a-teacher-but-that-doesn't-
mean-you-know-anything sort of voice. 'But
this is a very important point. The *accepted*
opinion is that she was this tragic figure, living
a solitary life in a remote parsonage with a

fanatical father, a mad brother and strange sisters. But she *liked* it. She *didn't like* people. She didn't want fame or renown. She even decided to die when she did. She'd had enough. She wouldn't even let them fetch the doctor!'

'Well, Tracey,' sighed Mrs Goldstein.

Alexa, this is what it's like having the Brain of Britain in your class. A great big clever cloggs who thinks it's her duty to challenge all the teachers on every single point. And you'd think our band of enlighteners would like this – get some stimulating discussion going, be mentally notching up the GCSEs on their credentials. But they don't. And they don't like it because she's CLEVERER THAN THEM! Yes, amazing as it might seem, Tracey Mann is cleverer than the combined brains of the whole academia of Langley Street High. It gets on their nerves. And it gets on our nerves too, I can tell you. Anyway, the reason I'm telling you this is that it's got me thinking. We're doing the poems of Emily Brontë so we can get a more 'in depth' look at *Wuthering Heights*. Mrs Goldstein is dead keen on what she calls 'getting to grips with the background story behind the story', which doesn't sound too bad in theory but is downright ear-buzzingly boring in the reality. So I was sitting there thinking that listening to bees droning would be more stimulating than Mrs Goldstein's squeaky ramblings, when I suddenly heard the lines:

Then I did check the tears of useless passion,
Weaned my young soul from yearning after thine;

I mean, how close can you get! Emily must have had a secret love, like me! But her tortured yearnings were channelled into literature and she became a genius. And then it all became clear; my die was cast, the seeds were sown. I would do the same! Pour the thwarted passion of a thousand lost moments into words and make my mark as one of the youngest lyric poets of all time.

Then Mrs Goldstein almost spoilt it all by saying that Emily's love poems were all made up and that she never so much as looked at a man. But then I thought, How would *she* know? She wasn't living next door, was she? And even if she had been, Emily would hardly be nipping round every five minutes to exchange confidences over tea and barm cakes with someone with a frizzy perm and a squeaky voice. Well would she?

And while I sat there I was already working on my first creation. I could hardly wait to get home to get started.

The problem, though, which became patently clear when I got back, is that it's all right if you've got 'barren hills' and 'cornfields all a-waving' and 'purple heath' and 'moonless misty domes' for inspiration. It's all right if you've got those in abundance, and some left over to spare. But what have you got if you live on Benbridge Estate? A few turd-ridden grass verges, a couple of seriously ill saplings in need of crutches, and a view from your bedroom window that looks like an airport runway lined with Monopoly houses. Hardly stuff to get the heart racing, to spew the creative juices forth. Benbridge has got less soul than the electrical goods department of the Co-op and it'll be something indeed if I manage to rise above it.

Anyway, I closed my curtains, put on my bedside light and meditated. I tried to shut out the buzz of the television and the distant drone of traffic and meditated on that star-crossed night. I won't mind if you think it's no good, Alexa. Don't be afraid to tell me the truth. There're few poets who haven't benefited from a bit of constructive criticism.

> *That fateful night that came and went*
> *The night he held her in his arms*
> *The night she thought that Heaven sent*
> *Him to conquer all her charms.*
> *Oh, cruel night! Rotten deceiver!*
> *How her vanity's been fed.*
> *He just thought he would relieve her*
> *When she fell and hurt her head.*

Alexa, let me know *exactly* what you think. Let me know if you think I've got a bit of promise. Poetry could be my ticket to salvation; my escape from the infinite path to certain gloom of spirit and mind.

Looking forward to hearing.

Yours

Gilly Freeborn

23 *Tudor Avenue*
Benbridge
Trowton TR0 9AF

Ms Alexa Deerheart   12 March
THE BIZZ

Dear Alexa

Thank you. It *was* my first, though. I've written
five more since that one – all love poems. I
looked up 'derivative' in the dictionary. It said:
'Taken from something else. Not radical or
original.' I suppose it's difficult not to let things
influence you though, to let other people's
thought patterns come into your mind. I've
bought a blue notebook to write in. I'll just
have to try to clear my brain and try to let the
'Freeborn' voice flow out.

I've been listening to the Contaminators on
my Walkman. I think it must be the kind of
stuff you have to listen to over and over again
before it grabs you. It just gives me a pain in
my ears at the moment. Most people in our
class are into the Greenhouse Boys but I think
they're pretty pathetic weeds. They just prance
around looking stupid singing stuff like 'How
could you leave me, Angel?' and 'Baby, baby,
baby, you're the one.' I mean, what's the point?
I don't know who I like really. I quite like The
Verve, but Rosalee likes them too, so of course

I can't say anything or she'll accuse me of copying. For some reason she thinks that my prime purpose in life, my ultimate aim, is to cultivate her tastes so I can become a sort of facsimile Rosalee Freeborn. That's what happens when your hugeous ego is all-consuming – you can't imagine anyone wanting to be anyone else.

Love's grip is tightening. I was in the corner shop after school on Thursday when I suddenly saw, two places in front of me, the back of HIS head, his glorious curls wisping. My legs went all funny again. They sort of turned jellinous and started wobbling and throbbing. I mean, he wasn't even doing anything, he was just standing there with a packet of sausages in his hand. I couldn't even see his face, but obviously his whole being is just potent and able to shoot out vibes to catch you unawares. I was actually having palpitations and had to put my hand on my heart to try to calm it down. And then he was gone.

I can't remember what happened next. All I know is that I left the shop empty-handed and found myself following him down Basingstoke Road. I had this compulsion to see where he lived, to know what sort of house sheltered his precious frame. As long as I kept a safe distance, I wasn't physically affected. I felt that the more I knew about him, the closer I would be. *Jonathan O'Neil lives at 49 Horseferries Road. It is a tall Victorian terraced house. His bedroom is in the attic. His mother has black hair too. They have a red car. There is a lilac bush in the front garden.* All this is poetry. I have written it in a special place at the back of my blue book.

Alexa, I suppose you think this is just a teenage crush. But surely no teenage crush ever felt like this. This is a real, strong, serious, full-blown *passion* that's invaded every vein, sinew, muscle, *bone*, in my body. It's embedded there like a diamond in a rock.

Yours

Gillian Freeborn

23 *Tudor Avenue*
Benbridge
Trowton TR0 9AF

Ms Alexa Deerheart   15 March
THE BIZZ

Dear Alexa

I've seen spotty Greg! It was half-past twelve
and I heard Rosalee's footsteps clicking up
Tudor Avenue accompanied by the barely dis-
cernible squeak of the Sportsbag's crepe-soled
shoes. I opened my curtains the tiniest fraction
of an inch to see them smooching up the road,
stopping every few seconds to gaze into each
other's eyes.

I knew that Mum was in her bedroom at
her lookout post behind the dressing table. She
never goes to sleep until Rosalee is safely
tucked up inside her 'Spring Daffodil' Habitat
sheets. I think this is a bit much, really: after
all, Rosalee is sixteen and a quarter. Still, at
least I know the score for when my time comes.

Anyway, when I heard Rosalee's key in the
lock I crept on to the landing and crouched
motionless behind the banisters. This is what
happened:

'You're GORGEOUS.' Grope, grope.

'Mmmmmmmm.' Wriggle, wriggle.

Long suction job with Rosalee pinned

against our Georgian Stripe wallpaper, standing on one leg. Lots of slobbery noises and groans from Greg. Then:

'Shhhhhh! Mum'll hear.'

'No she won't.' Followed by some dead-serious groping and squeaky little noises from Rosalee.

Then, 'You've got gorgeous breasts – like, like . . . soft melons!'

Well, that did it, I'm afraid. I've heard some funny things in my life but sometimes you just can't control yourself, can you? This bubble sort of shot through my chest and burst into my windpipe and came out in a snort of ear-shattering proportions.

'You little bitch!' cried Rosalee, leaping up the stairs two by two, to arrive at the same time as Mum coming out of her bedroom saying, 'What's all this noise? It's a quarter to one!' The light went on and the three of us all stared at poor thwarted Greg as if we were absolutely amazed he was there at all.

When Rosalee had recovered her composure she screeched, 'She's been spying on us, the little snot rag.'

'No I wasn't, I was just– '

'That's enough,' snapped Mum. 'Gillian, go back to bed. Rosalee, say goodnight to your boyfriend, and put out the lights. And don't forget to put the chain on the door.'

Well, he's not *too* bad really. Bit greasy, but I suppose these sporty types can't help it. He's quite tall, with mousy blond hair and skinny legs. The downside of this experience is that Rosalee is going to get her own back on me pretty soon, and in a big way. But it was worth it. It was absolutely worth it, because if she ever goes too far I've always got 'soft melons' to hurl at her. Yes, I've got that for years to come, so she'd better watch out.

Something I've learned from this is that men can be pretty pathetic when they're worked up into a passion. But one thing I'm sure of is that HE'd never say 'soft melons'. HE'd never say anything so downright daft in a million years.

Yours

Gilly Freeborn

23 Tudor Avenue
Benbridge
Trowton TR0 9AF

Ms Alexa Deerheart   17 March
THE BIZZ

Dear Alexa

Friday. I was on my way from maths to art yesterday, grappling about in my bag for my crayon case, when my hand touched something smooth and square. I looked quickly. Smooth, white, crisp and square. An envelope! An envelope that must have been *put there* in secret. My heart raced. I slipped into a deserted side corridor and took it out. It said:

Very private

To G. Freeborn

and there was A HEART, a small heart drawn carefully in red felt-tip pen. It's happened, I thought. Finally. I mean, such intense feeling loose in the atmosphere *must* find its target eventually. Well, that was what I thought.

I saved it up until the evening. After tea I went upstairs, sat on my bed, pulled the curtains, put on my bedside light and dug into my

55

bag. Eyes closed, I pulled out the envelope and ran my fingers over its sharp contours.

I opened the envelope very slowly, being careful not to tear it, and pulled out a folded sheet *with writing inside*. I closed my eyes. Maybe it said, 'Gilly, I love you' or 'Gilly, I have watched and waited for too long' or 'Gillian, I don't know how to say this, but something is happening to me. . . .'

Slowly, slowly, I opened the paper. The three scrawly lines sent a sack of potatoes from my heart to my stomach.

Meet me behind the craft room tomorrow at 4.

Sined, W (you know who!)

I should have known. Tricked by false hope, fooled. Wayne Cross! Dribbling, piddling Wayne Cross. Snotty, spitty sniveller. I felt stupid, low down. I suppose when you think about it, Alexa, would someone of perfect physical beauty and high mind fall in love with a short, stubby, unformed adolescent? Why should they?

Wayne Cross. Well, he can wait outside the craft room until the cows die. He can find

56

someone else to snort and dribble over. If he thinks I enjoyed that tortuous slobbering, the arrogance of men must be above anything.

Yours in disgust

Gilly Freeborn

PS   In fact, this was just what I needed to propel me into action re the next LSHYWAC meeting. It's going to be two weeks on Wednesday. I made a poster saying 'WHAT DO MEN THINK WE ARE?' and put it up all over the school. I wonder if Annie'll come.

23 Tudor Avenue
Benbridge
Trowton TR0 9AF

Ms Alexa Deerheart   20 March
THE BIZZ

Dear Alexa

Something's going on at home. At first I
thought everyone was getting fed up of having
to be at work/school/college during these slow
muggy days. But two things have happened to
make me wonder if there's not more to it. I
mean, see what you think.

Last night we were all together (a rare
occurrence) sitting on our Edwardian Stripe
plush Dralon suite watching 'The Dark Night
Cometh' which is this goosepimpling thriller
we're all addicted to (have you seen it? It's
fantastic) when the doorbell rang. Mum looked
at Dad and Dad just kept staring at the television as if to say, ''snothing to do with me, I
just live here.'

And Mum just continued sitting there too,
with the doorbell screeching and Rosalee and
me wondering who on earth this unwelcome
visitor could be. Then Mum said, 'Bet I know
who *that* is,' in this funny croaky under-the-
breath voice and padded out to the door
looking as if she was expecting the missing link

and his brother inviting themselves to dinner. Then we heard, 'Hi, Michelle! God, I thought the bell had broken,' and we knew it was Auntie Paula. Then Mum said, 'It's your *sister*,' in the voice she uses for announcing she's found a slug in the lettuce. Auntie Paula is Dad's younger sister and even though Mum's always saying that she's an 'overgrown teenager who ought to get her act together' we think she's great – well, I do anyway. She always cheers us up because she does such amazing things.

And Auntie Paula tumbled into the lounge and kissed us and Dad, and dropped her bags on the floor and I thought, Good, she's coming to stay. But Mum disappeared upstairs and didn't come down *the whole evening*! Dad got out a bottle of wine and made us all sandwiches. Auntie Paula told us how she'd been fined for selling her sculptured candles on the underground and how she'd had a row with her boyfriend, Tom, who'd thrown her out, even though it was *her* flat. And she said could she stay for just a few days while she got her head together? And Dad said fine, she could sleep on the sofa. Then they got talking about the old days when they went to all-night concerts and demonstrations and stuff and about how Dad had been arrested for holding a vampire party on his roof and gave his name as Gordon Undead, which is one of my favourite stories of all time.

Then later on in bed I heard Mum and Dad arguing in undertones.

The second thing that happened was that this evening someone put a pamphlet through our door. Not normally a noteworthy event, but Dad picked it up, went purple in the face and ran after the poor pamphleteer shouting, 'Don't you dare put this rubbish through MY letterbox,' and 'Who's given you the *right*,' and 'Who do you bloody well think you are?' It turned out to be a party political broadsheet on behalf of the Conservative candidate for the Benbridge area who's been campaigning to turn the wild open space at the end of our road into a posh private health club. And our neighbour, Hugh Parkinson, who was pruning his hedge, dropped his shears while the pamphleteer ran down Tudor Avenue with hundreds of Piers Bowen Smiths trailing from him like snowflakes. And Dad started picking them up and screwing them into balls and shouting, 'Here you bloody well are, you self-satisfied load of... FAT BUMS!' and chucking them into people's gardens!

Mum just hid behind the door until he came in. And when he did she went white in the face and said, 'What are you trying to *do* to me, Gordon? Have you gone *completely* mad?' in this very slow deliberate voice. And, quite honestly, Alexa, we were all wondering the same thing, except for Auntie Paula who said, 'Right on, Gordon!'

Well, Alexa, pretty weird, eh? I know my parents are politically opposed, but this seems a bit extreme, don't you think? Do you think my Dad is becoming unhinged? In any case, it seems there's something up with my parents.

Yours in perplexion

Gilly Freeborn

PS   I've been so depressed, so cast down, that I've almost forgotten that it's my birthday in three weeks' time. At last. No more of this 'nearly fourteen' stuff. I'll be there – on the great white way to adulthood. *Fourteen* really does sound well, viable, don't you think? I mean, in only a few months I'll be 'nearly fifteen', won't I!

23 *Tudor Avenue*
Benbridge
Trowton TR0 9AF

Ms Alexa Deerheart   25 March
THE BIZZ

Dear Alexa

It was Good Friday yesterday. Auntie Paula
came down town with me to 'see how the other
half lives' and to buy a tape of 'The Mind
Music of Eugene Organ' whoever he is. She
kept saying 'heavens above' and 'God save us,
what *are* they doing to our towns' as we walked
past the tenth washing machine shop. She
didn't go much on the Arndale Centre either.
She called it a 'tomb for the living dead' and
said, 'I don't know how you can live here, Gilly.
I don't know how you *can*. Gordon must be
off his rocker to live in a place like this.' And I
told her about my plans to be a poet and how
hard it was to get inspired by squares and rec-
tangles and new trees that were hardly trees at
all. 'I know what you mean, Gilly,' she sighed.
'I know what you mean.'

So I took her to the Fresh Bake, which at
least opens out on to a real street with paving
stones. We had doughnuts and espresso coffee
and she started telling me about Tom, and how
they needed space to 'sort their heads out' and

62

how she had to do all the cooking and washing, which simply wasn't fair, especially as she had to make about a hundred sculptured candles a week just to break even. 'Don't let this happen to you, Gilly,' she said. 'Don't fall into the trap. In fact, I wouldn't even learn to cook, if I were you.' And I told her that there wasn't much chance of that anyway, remembering my dismal collapsed-tomato experience. And then it all just sort of came out. I told her about my weeks of turmoil, of hopes born and hopes dashed. About Judy Fry and Annie, and the party, and when I got to the stuffed-tomato episode she just exploded, which was a shame as she had a mouth full of Fresh Bake Double Jam Doughnut Special which is pretty difficult to control at the best of times. Anyway, it suddenly seemed like the funniest thing that had happened in the history of the world and I began laughing too and in the end we were both CONVULSED over our table and in danger of losing our doughnuts altogether. That's the thing about Auntie Paula, she always makes you see the funny side of things.

We were laughing so much I didn't hear the door open and when I came to, Annie and her mum were walking by our table. 'Hi,' I said. 'Hmm,' said Annie, giving me that horrible sideways sneer and sticking her head in the air. 'Oh, hello, Gillian,' said Annie's mum enthusiastically. 'We haven't seen much of you these days.' It was all horribly embarrassing with

Annie's mum standing there smiling and Annie trying to pull her away by the sleeve and Auntie Paula and I red in the face from laughing so much.

I couldn't help watching Annie out of the corner of my eye. I really wished we were sitting together and I had to stop myself going over to make it up there and then because Auntie Paula had cheered me up so much it all seemed rather stupid.

Auntie Paula told me she was going back on Monday. 'Well, I'm not exactly helping the situation,' she said. And I asked what she meant and she said, 'Adults have their problems, too, Gilly. It'll work itself out.'

So, Alexa, I suppose she was talking about Mum and Dad, and Dad being so strange these days. But I didn't ask. Somehow I felt it was something I didn't want to know.

Before she goes, she's going to help me with my LSHYWAC speech. She takes me seriously, which is more than some people in the world. I'm really sad she's going back.

Yours

Gilly Freeborn

23 *Tudor Avenue*
Benbridge
Trowton TR0 9AF

Ms Alexa Deerheart   3 April
THE BIZZ

Dear Alexa

Back at school and I'm feeling low, low, low. Everything seems pretty hopeless. Judy's been saying that they're planning to go ON HOLIDAY together. Well, anyway, that her family is going to the south of France and HE's going with them. That sounds like serious stuff to me. Sometimes I can hardly believe we're the same age. Every day she seems to look more sophisticated, more, well, stunning, though I hate to say it. She also seems to have an unlimited wardrobe – she's been coming to school in the most *amazing* outfits making us all feel like puny adolescents, which I suppose we are in comparison. And everywhere you look *there they are*, hand in hand or arm in arm, and Judy never misses an opportunity to tell us that they've done this or done that and I suppose pretty well everyone in our class has given up, except for me, who just *can't*.

This is real love, and it's like a pain made up of frustration and jealousy and thwarted hope all together. I keep thinking that if he got to know me, saw through the outer shell to the *inner soul*; knew that I had ideals, wrote lyric poetry and had *deep feelings*, he'd throw Judy Fry over in a moment for she never does anything but preen herself and prance around looking pretty. What on earth they *talk about*, I can't imagine.

So, well, I was prowling the playground after lunch pretending to look for someone but really hoping for a glimpse of HIM unfettered by HER and my efforts were rewarded because, in desperation, I wandered on to the playing fields and there he was playing football. Oh, heavens! His long legs *bounded* across the field, his hair *flew* in the wind. And just watching him made me go wobbly all over. I stood at the back of a small band of spectators and experienced half an hour of pure unadulterated BLISS and all the time I was thinking, HE's touched me. He's *picked me up* and *held me in his arms*. There must be some hope, somehow.

Luckily, I had my copy of W. H. in my pocket so I sat down on the grass and pretended to read while watching them pack up out of the corner of my eye. It's the way he *moves* that gets me: he takes long, light strides, as if he's walking on air – he sort of *flows*.

The bell went. I had the sudden realization that he was coming towards me, so I stuck my head inside my book and affected a look of deep concentration. All the time my heart was banging away in my chest, going *boom, boom, boom,* like Big Ben at midnight. My face was flushing deep purple. I could feel it glowing red-hot, and my hands were shaking so much they could hardly hold the book and I started *sweating* and my eye started *twitching* and I thought, Oh God, I'm going to *explode* right here on the playing field of Langley Street High.

Then I felt a rush of air as he bent down to pick up his black Puma sportsbag and by this time I was such a gibbering wreck I was almost having *convulsions* and I felt sure I was visibly *gyrating* like a pneumatic spin-dryer.

And he was standing next to me, wiping his arms with a towel and taking deep breaths and I was thinking, I don't think I can actually stand this much longer when he said, 'Oh, hello. You a football fan?'

I was forced to look up, though I couldn't look him straight in the eye, and I replied, 'Oh, yeah,' almost jumping out of my own skin with the surprise of being able to speak at all.

'Well,' said he. 'That's great. We could do with as much support as we can get. See you.' And he floated off, the wispy bits of hair at the back of his neck dancing in the wind, leaving me in a cloud of exhausted euphoria and it was some time before my body felt back together enough to make its way to home ec where I spent an hour whisking up some gunge that was supposed to be the flesh and blood of a

Victoria sponge but which, when cooked, looked like a cowpat with a fatal injury. And, I thought, who cares?

On the way home my spirits started plummeting again. I replayed the scene a hundred times in my mind for hidden meanings in 'You a football fan?' and 'See you' but, of course, there were none. He was just being polite, wasn't he? I just happened to be there and he felt obliged to speak. I could have been anybody.

And by the time I got home I felt about as cheerful as my cowpat Victoria sponge which I hurled into the bin in a fury of self-loathing.

Alexa, I need to raise my self-esteem. I've got two aims: to give a triumphant performance at our LSHYWAC meeting and to write the prizewinning essay on W. H. If I can't win him with my beauty, I'll try to do it with my intelligence and wit, such as they are.

Yours in dejection

Gillian Freeborn

23 Tudor Avenue
Benbridge
Trowton TR0 9AF

Ms Alexa Deerheart   6 April
THE BIZZ

Dear Alexa

Wednesday has come and gone. We had the best LSHYWAC meeting we've ever had. I spent all Tuesday night working on my speech – which was pretty good, even though I say it myself. Auntie Paula had given me some new perspectives and I based the whole thing on 'words mean action' which means there's no point sitting around talking about what should be happening and then going away and doing nothing at all.

I'd just finished breakfast and was putting the finishing touches to my summing-up when I sensed this 'presence' behind me. In other words I could smell Rosalee's sickly sweet Midnight Passion wafting about my nostrils and I realized with horror that she'd been standing over me eyeballing every word. Really! I don't know what she finds so irresistibly interesting about my private world – she probably thought I was writing some really hot stuff in my five-year lockable secret diary. She was disappointed, but she couldn't resist a chance to put me down.

'God! What a load of rubbish. Who do you think you are? A budding Mrs Pankhurst . . . except that you haven't got any buds!' And she seemed to find this so rib-ticklingly funny that she nearly collapsed on the floor she was snorting so much. Pathetic!

And Mum said, 'Can't you two girls leave each other alone for five minutes,' which was hardly fair as I'd be quite happy if Rosalee left me alone for ever and went to live with Sportsbag in some remote region of outer Milton Keynes, or some other place where nobody in their right minds would want to go.

Anyway, Rosalee went off to college (she's doing office management, which is just another name for being a grovelling secretary, although Rosalee thinks it sounds dead posh). And Mum said, 'What are you writing, Gillian?' And I said it was just something for school; which was true. I don't see why I should turn my private thoughts inside out for my family to examine at their leisure, do you?

Sarryan and I sat together during break and began drawing up our plans. We had six points, or rather I did. Sarryan didn't seem to be concentrating; she kept looking at Michael Barnes and pulling faces. Sometimes, I don't think Sarryan takes LSHYWAC seriously enough. In fact, sometimes I think I'm one of the few people in this school whose mind has the ability to stretch beyond boys and rock bands. Even since the arrival of HIM, I've still managed to keep a few brain cells free for more intellectual musings, difficult though it's been, I can tell you.

Anyway, this is what we came up with:

1. Girls-only computer days

2. Women's studies compulsory for both sexes!

3. All sports to be open to both sexes

4. Girls no longer prepared to make food and do decorations for the annual open night (bloody cheek!). This year it is to be the responsibility of the boys and after that, shared.

'Can you think of anything else?' I asked Sarryan in a loud voice, as Annie was sitting two tables down talking to Tracey Mann.

'Uh, dunno ... well, how about *co-educational* CHANGING ROOMS!' she screeched and then burst into hysterical laughter.

'Shhhhh!' I hissed. But too late. Michael Barnes and half of 11a had heard, not to mention Annie and Brainbox who were throwing each other what-can-you-expect looks. I felt sick.

'Yeah, great idea!' said runner bean Barnes. 'You can share my towel anytime, sweetie!' Which is just the sort of pathetic, chauvinist remark that I'm campaigning against.

'Be serious,' I said, furious. 'This is important.'

'Well, I'm all for a bit of radical action,' said Sarryan. 'Let's say six is that if they refuse to discuss our demands we'll . . . go on strike, or something.'

So that was point six. But somehow my faith in Sarryan's integrity had been shaken.

As we made our way to geography (I hate Wednesday mornings – geography, then *maths*) Annie walked by arm in arm with Brainbox Tracey. 'Are you going to this *meeting* tonight?' Tracey was saying. 'Well, maybe,' replied Annie. 'It'll be interesting to see what *some people* have to say.' And I knew they were both smiling silly sniggery little sideways smiles at my back, which only made me even more determined to be a success. I was thinking how amazing it was that only a few weeks ago we had been best friends, inseparable, sharing our innermost thoughts and feelings, talking about one day getting a flat together, in fact, being together for ever, and *laughing* about stuck-up brainbox show-offs like Tracey Mann who Annie now evidently thought was the bee's knees with knobs on. Hypocrite! I'm beginning to discover that there are very few people in the world who mean what they say, deep down. I'm glad I found out in time, I can tell you.

Geography was dire. We spent the whole lesson depositing mineral wealth on a map of Australia in the form of red blobs. My mind just switched off, like a light. Maths was worse. Mr Parkins said that if I couldn't even grasp the fundamentals I hadn't the hope of a GCSE and 'you'd better get down to some serious work, Gillian Freeborn, if you want to make something of yourself.' And I was thinking, Just you wait, just wait.

At last the bell went. I grabbed Sarryan and Em, picked up my notes and strode purposefully into the craft room. There were TEN people there. I must say I felt really nervous. Annie and Tracey sat at the back, Em sat at the front and Sarryan sat next to me at the top table. There were two girls from 10c and *five* others from our class: Ellen Pugh, Alice Crayford, Ranesh Japoor, Winnie Pack and, of course, Phyllis Bean, who nearly put me off my stride by smiling inanely at me through the whole meeting and simultaneously sucking a disgusting stick of licorice which was sending little streams of brown spit down her chin.

I launched straight into my speech about how things really hadn't changed much in the past twenty years, and how girls were still expected to do the same sort of grot stuff they'd been doing for centuries, like cooking and cleaning up after men, and it was about time something was done about it and we could begin to change things by campaigning in this very school, and not just *talking* but *taking action* if they don't listen, because we were absolutely *justified* in our demands and it was about time people realized it. And then I read out our demands and we discussed them one by one. And neither Annie nor Tracey said a word. There was nothing they could say, really – I was so fired up and confident because everyone was actually *listening* and not making daft remarks.

When it was over they all crowded round me saying, 'Well done, Gilly,' and stuff like that. I felt *fantastic*. I suddenly realized that if you feel serious about something, everyone else will feel serious about it too, and we were all just about ready to go and confront Pennings right there and then, except that he had gone home hours ago, for it was half-past five and the time had just *flown*.

And I was thinking, Annie'll be eating her words now, feeling how she'd been unfair and too quick to judge her serious-minded and pro-found-thinking best friend. I looked for her because I felt sure she'd want to be making up. But she'd gone! On my way out with Sarryan and Emily I saw her striding down the corridor with her arm round Tracey. Ugh! Well, I'd proved that I had real integrity and motivation and if she couldn't even see that, she wasn't worth it. Still, I bet she's regretting everything now; pretty soon she'll come crawling back to *me* and then I'll tell her to get lost, maybe.

I walked home in the twilight feeling marvellous, which was a novel experience after the last few weeks. And I was thinking how everyone would be wanting to join LSHYWAC now; now we were really doing something. And that HE would get to hear about this intelligent, imaginative girl who was motivating the whole school, firing everyone with enthusiasm, battling against the establishment which was hanging on to outdated, outmoded ideas.

I typed up our demands on Rosalee's typewriter and we handed them into Pennings yesterday. 'Well, girls,' he said. 'It's nice to see you taking some initiative. We'll give this some serious thought.'

'I hope so, Mr Pennings,' I replied. 'We've got a lot of support.'

'He'll need a *bit* of time,' I said to Sarryan afterwards. 'We'll give him till half term to get something moving.'

Alexa, I'm really feeling a lot better about myself after all this. I only hope I can keep it up.

Yours inspired

Gillian Freeborn

23 *Tudor Avenue*
Benbridge
Trowton TR0 9AF

Ms Alexa Deerheart   11 April
THE BIZZ

Dear Alexa

It was my birthday yesterday, though you'd
hardly have known it. In the deep recesses of
my mind I suppose I thought something marvellous might take place, like a trumpet chorus
or even just Rosalee being normal for once.
But all that happened was that my neck swelled
up and Mum made me stay in bed because she
thought I was getting glandular fever. Really!
And even though Mum and Dad brought me
up a special birthday breakfast and sat on my
bed making jokes, I felt downright miserable
and low. Not least, Alexa, because I'd been
hinting for the past three months that I wanted
a metallic cross-over bag that I'd seen in Top
Shop. I'd pointed it out to Mum at least three
million zillion times saying things like, 'Wow!
imagine having that,' and 'What a fantastic
colour!' and 'Hey, it's *only* fifteen pounds.' But
obviously her psyche isn't tuned in to my
thoughts and desires, or she's just forgotten
what it's like to be fourteen years old.

      You know what I got? A briefcase! A blue

canvas *briefcase*. I might have guessed they'd give me something for school. Something *useful*. And it took a *huge* effort to pretend to look pleased, I can tell you. But what else could I do with Dad sitting there grinning all over his face and saying, 'Look it's got a pocket for this and a pocket for that and it's even got a special holder for your *ruler*.' Oh, *great*, Dad, thanks.

Rosalee gave me a cheapo bottle of bath foam called Blue Lagoon, saying 'Now you won't need to go nicking mine,' and a birthday card which had 'To my dear Grandad' on it. For heaven's sake. You'd think she'd have tried to make a bit of an effort, tried to do things with a bit of grace. After all, it's not every day that you hit the big ONE FOUR, is it?

My glands went down this morning. Mum said it must have been a freak virus. Typical, I thought. Ordinary viruses are for normal people. I have to get the freak kind. The kind that manifests itself out of spite just to ruin what should have been one of the best days of the year.

Anyway, I cheered up a bit when I got to school. Em and Sarry had made me a card saying:

> *Gillian is one year older*
> *So she will be feeling bolder*
> *'Cos she'll never be thirteen again*
> *Love from Sarry, love from Em.*

Then in English Mrs Goldstein got everyone to sing 'Happy Birthday for Yesterday' which was funny and nice. Anyway, I'm here now, Alexa. There's no going back. It's onwards and upwards from now on!

Love

Gillian Freeborn (aged 14)

23 Tudor Avenue
Benbridge
Trowton TR0 9AF

Ms Alexa Deerheart   12 April
THE BIZZ

Dear Alexa

Something's happening! My God, I can hardly believe it really is. Alexa, can it be true? I'd better tell you everything, in detail, just in case.

Was woken this morning by the usual brutal curtain-ripping method. Bend down to lift up my cup of tea and . . . felt a sort of achy, stretchy pain in the side of my chest. My first thought was that I'd ruptured myself during one of my soul-searching dreams. But after I'd finished my toast and Marmite downstairs and had listened to Rosalee gibbering on about Mitzi (bet that's not her real name) at ZAP and how she'd got real style and how much she was teaching Rosalee about the nuances of the fashion world, it was still there! And by the time I got to school it had spread *across my chest* and during netball it was really quite *uncomfortable* and I was just beginning to get really fed up with it when I realized that it was probably, in all likelihood, *a growing pain*!!!

So I said to Sarryan, casually, 'I've got this funny pain just *here*,' and she said, ''sprobably a *growing pain*; is it all achy – a sort of stretchy feeling?' And, Alexa, that's exactly what it's like and Sarryan should know as she's had her bosoms for *ages* and obviously knows the whole process inside out.

Well, Alexa, I'd never have thought I'd actually be grateful to be walking around with a pain throbbing away in my chest but really it looks pretty well certain that things are happening, that the hormones are finally on the move. How long will it take before they start showing? Do you think I'll have proper bosoms in time for the summer holidays? How long does it take from this stage? Will they come all at once or will they start gradually and then just burst forth? Write soon. I need precise, accurate information.

Yours

Gilly Freeborn

23 *Tudor Avenue*
Benbridge
Trowton TR0 9AF

Ms Alexa Deerheart   16 April
THE BIZZ

Dear Alexa

Patience, patience! I know everyone is different. I know, I know, I know. I just need a bit of reassurance, that's all. I have to be sure that the process has started. That there's reason to hope.

Went down town with Sarryan and Emily yesterday. Emily was buying some new shoes. Her mum had given her THIRTY POUNDS to buy what she liked. Really, sometimes I think I was short-changed when the mums were dished out. Mine would *never* give me thirty pounds to buy *anything*; she'd insist on coming with me to make sure I didn't buy any 'rubbish' – which means anything with the slightest bit of cred. And she'd stand over me saying things like, 'Are you sure they *fit* properly, Gillian?' and '*They* look nice!' trying to steer me towards some hideous 'sensible' shoes with 'plenty of toe room'.

Anyway, we went to Shoe Shapes where I jealously watched Emily buy a pair of red sandals with crepe soles, and then Sarryan wanted to buy some fishnet tights so we went to the tomb of the living dead to look in Top Shop where I saw this fantastic blue leather jacket. Emily said to try it on, so I did. And even though I say it myself, it really suited me. Sarry said it made me look at least seventeen. But it was fifty-five pounds and suddenly the hopelessness of the situation hit me. Even if I could drag Mum in here, and even if some miracle had happened and she was willing to splash out her hard-earned cash on me, she would be saying, 'Fifty-five pounds for *that*! Gillian, really; it wouldn't last you two minutes, look – it's just been *thrown* together. Let's go to Marks, I'm sure we can find something just as nice.' See, Alexa, this is what I'm up against in my efforts to gain credibility in the world of the cool and fashionable.

So Emily had her sandals and Sarry had her fishnets and I had absolutely nothing at all except £1.65 which we spent in the Fresh Bake on two doughnuts and a hot chocolate between the three of us. And I decided I needed to get some money of my own; I'd get a Saturday job, like Rosalee.

THEN, on the way home we were walking past Hair Now when I just happened to look inside. 'My God!' I squeaked, grabbing hold of Emily's arm. 'Look, *look*!' It was HIM. I couldn't see his face but I saw his long brown legs, as familiar to me as my own short white ones, and the black Adidas trainers left no room for doubt. THERE HE WAS, trapped and vulnerable, having his hair washed by a short, spotty girl in green dungarees.

'This must be where he gets his hair cut,' said Em, employing her extraordinary powers of perception. And the three of us just stood there, staring. It seemed impossible that HE could be so sort of . . . exposed.

Then out of the corner of my eye I saw a notice in the window. 'Saturday junior required immediately – apply within.' I kept quiet about it, just in case Sarry or Em might have the same idea. I was going all wibbly wobbly at the possibilities. It seemed as if Fate had read my thoughts and decided to solve the two most pressing problems of my life in one swoop. When we finally dragged ourselves away, Em said, 'Well, I suppose Judy's got the whole thing sewn up, worse luck.' And Sarryan said, 'What's she got that we haven't,' which no one bothered to answer. Anyway, Sarryan's been going out with Michael Barnes, so I don't suppose she feels that desperate.

I pretended to wait for my bus while they went their separate ways, and when they were safely out of sight I tore back to Hair Now, checked that HE had gone, took a deep breath and went inside to ask about the job. A tall, dark man called Mr Giorgio asked me how old I was and whether I was 'a gooda hard worker' and did I know that people like a 'hard rubbin' gooda stronga shampooa' and not a 'flippyfloppy strokin' like zeez' and he pulled a face and flopped his wrists about to demonstrate. 'Of course, I know that,' I said. 'I wash everybody's hair at home.' A lie, but Love makes you bold.

Well, I got the job. And Alexa, pretty soon I could be giving HIM 'a hard rubbin' gooda stronga shampoo'; running my fingers through his glorious locks; talking to him about whether he wants conditioner or not, and . . . well I'm sure I can think of other things. What Mum'll say about it I don't know. She's been pretty keen on me spending Saturdays locked up in my room revising maths or geography or some other tortuous subject that I've got behind on. Well, too bad. It's done now, and you can't let people down, can you?

Mum was fine. Surprise, surprise. She said it was a good idea for me to get some work experience, as long as I made up the time for studying. But, quite frankly, maths and geography are the last things on my mind. Who needs them!

Yours

Gillian Freeborn

PS   Do you think there are many feminist hairdressers? I mean, is hairdressing an OK thing to be doing? I had a crisis of conscience in the middle of the night. I

woke up thinking, Well, it's a pretty
menial sort of job, even though it is only
part-time. Then I thought, There're
plenty of *men* in the business so it's not
like being a secretary or a *nanny* or
something. Still, I think I'll keep quiet
about it at school. You never know. I
don't want to damage my cool.

23 *Tudor Avenue*
Benbridge
Trowton TR0 9AF

Ms Alexa Deerheart   18 April
THE BIZZ

Dear Alexa

I don't know why Rosalee hates me so much. I
don't hate her, not really. She *can't* be jealous
of me – she's got everything, as far as I can
see: she's left school, she's got a trendy Saturday job, lots of clothes, a boyfriend (of sorts)
and breasts. I sometimes think she's prettier
than me, too, although it's difficult to tell. I
don't know how I'm going to turn out *exactly*
as some bits are obviously still growing, but
her hair is a browny blonde whereas mine is
just plain browny brown, worse luck.

Yesterday she was getting ready to go to a
concert with Greg. The Spitz were playing two
gigs at the Screen Underground (which sounds
like a pretty funky venue but which is really
just the cinema in the basement of the grotty
Arndale). They must have had a serious lapse
of cool to come here, that's all I can say.

Anyway, it was one of those horrible rainy
Mondays where you're standing in the kitchen
staring in the mirror at a face that the fluor-
escent light has turned a dismal shade of

86

undercooked Cornish pasty, and the rain is pitting against the window somehow reminding you that there's nothing out there but the flat lands of Benbridge Estate, with the streetlamps throwing out their puny beams on the new tarmac and the sun-scorched grass verges from which hardly even a dandelion can sprout without an indestructible instinct to survive. I was standing there feeling as if my life had as much excitement as a fairground goldfish's and thinking, Emily Brontë never had to suffer this slow murder of mind and spirit. No, she could just *leap* out on to the moors and straight into 'rose trees wet with dew' and 'tower like rocks' and 'slopes where the north wind is raving' and stuff like that. And I was thinking that I'd go upstairs and get stuck into *Wuthering Heights* (I've reached the bit where Heathcliff is trying to marry off poor sickly Linton to unsuspecting Cathy) when Rosalee came bouncing in all dolled up and full of anticipation of an exciting evening, making me feel about a million times worse.

'Admiring yourself again,' she threw at me snottily.

'Why not,' I replied. 'I'm such a raving beauty.' But, really, Alexa, I felt as beautiful as the uglier ugly sister with Rosalee sitting there in her new ZAP metallic-silver dress and black patent mules.

'Would you like to come?' she said suddenly.

I could hardly believe my ears, but already Monday evening was changing course and I was fantasizing telling Sarry and Em all about what a rave-up it had been. 'Cor, yeah,' I said with pathetic uninhibited enthusiasm.

'Shame,' said Rosalee. 'They don't let kids in!'

Just at that moment, Mum came through the door saying, 'Why *not* take Gillian with you?' the surprise of which nearly knocked me over. 'I'm sure she'll be all right. How much are the tickets?'

'For God's sake,' said Rosalee, as if she'd been asked to eat live maggots. 'I'm not taking *her* with me. Mum *please*. I'm going with Greg and we don't want her with us, showing us up.'

'Well, he wouldn't mind, would he?' persevered Mum. 'Who are these Spitz, anyway?'

'No, he wouldn't mind,' I added, now desperate to escape this miserable Monday and get a bit of excitement.

'*You've* got a real nerve,' said Rosalee. '*Remember*, Greg hates you. He thinks you're a snot-nosed little creep *spy*.'

Well, Alexa, I suppose she had a point, hadn't she? That was a pretty low down thing I did to them and I made up my mind there and then to try to be genuinely extra nice to Rosalee in the future. Foster some sisterly love. Then Mum sighed, 'Well, OK, Rosie. Though Gilly *is* fourteen now and you could start doing more things together.'

The possibilities of this statement suddenly seemed very attractive. Rosalee could be my key to a less restricted life. I'd just have to work on it, very hard.

So, sentenced to the gloomy night, I finally went upstairs and got stuck into W. H. If I closed my eyes, I could really imagine the raging, storm-wrecked branches and the fierce anger of Heathcliff's passion as he prowled the moors in search of his lost love. And I felt like crying out, 'I know how you feel, mate. I know how you feel!'

Before I turned off the light, I started another poem:

> *Oh, gloominous, rain-washed night!*
> *That sucks my spirit drear....*

That's as far as I got. Somehow, there was nothing more to be said.

Yours drearily

Gilly Freeborn

23 Tudor Avenue
Benbridge
Trowton TR0 9AF

Ms Alexa Deerheart   20 April
THE BIZZ

Dear Alexa

Got home yesterday to find Dad sitting at the dining room table going through some old photographs. 'Look, Gilly,' he said. 'Mum. If only you'd known her then. She was full of ideas and so creative. We had IDEALS. We were going to buy a farm in Wales and raise our kids barefoot among the cows and chickens. Now look what we've come to. Look what we've *come to!*' And he stared up at our crystal-drop mini chandelier and burst into tears.

And I began thinking that it'd have been quite nice living on a farm, with Mum waving to us from an ivy-framed door and me dancing around barefoot among the chickens, and maybe Rosalee milking a cow. And I burst into tears, too, at the thought of this lost childhood paradise. At that moment the key went in the lock and Rosalee popped round the door to find us both blubbing away like babies.

'Dad,' I said after she'd beaten a quick retreat. 'Is anything wrong? You 'n' Mum aren't going to split up, are you?' I could hardly believe that I was saying it, outright.

'Life is never straightforward, Gillykins,' he said. 'You'll find that out when you grow up.'

Alexa, all these ghastly things I'm going to find out when I grow up, like sex and people not turning out to be the people you thought they were and arguing all the time or, worse, not speaking at all.

Do you think my dad's thinking of leaving home? I can't bear the thought. Surely he wouldn't leave us. Where would he go? Who will keep Mum under control? Do you think he could even be having an affair with some idealistic young girl with long hair?

I watched Mum and Dad closely that evening. They hardly spoke. Dad cooked dinner and then put his headphones on and just lay on the sofa, even though part six of 'The Dark Night Cometh' was on.

Later on I said to Rosalee, 'Mum 'n' Dad don't seem very happy. Do you think it's serious?' After all, a problem shared is a problem shared.

But Rosalee said, 'They're just having a few problems, snotbag. And it's none of your business.'

Alexa, it seems that number 23 Tudor Avenue is a boiling pot of suppressed emotions. One day soon we're going to explode!

Yours

Gilly Freeborn

23 Tudor Avenue
Benbridge
Trowton TR0 9AF

Ms Alexa Deerheart   23 April
THE BIZZ

Dear Alexa

Suspended animation! 'Temporary cessation of the outward signs and of some of the functions of life.' This is what I've been having. I suppose that I've got so much going on inside my head that the world needs to stop for a while to try to catch up. I keep going into these sort of *trances*, fantasies where anything can happen.

I'm on an aeroplane, Concorde. HE is sitting next to me, he's reading *Wuthering Heights*, totally absorbed. He doesn't notice me. I'm wearing Rosalee's metallic-silver dress with a feather boa; my hair is really long and thick and is flowing down my shoulders like waterfalls. We're flying over the Indian Ocean. All of a sudden, the plane begins to shudder and jerk. 'Fasten your seat belts' lights up above our heads. 'Do not panic,' comes over the intercom in serious tones. 'Prepare for an emergency landing.' People start to panic immediately, except for me, and HIM. He turns, puts down his book. His eyes meet mine.

92

Big, brown, liquid eyes. There's a moment of recognition. We stare at each other, long and hard. Time stops. 'You,' he says. 'It's you.' Instant love spasms. The plane judders like mad, a wing falls off. But we don't notice – flames leap about us, our lips touch. . . .

And then I was back on the number 43a to the library, sitting next to a blubbery fat man in a suit who smelt of fish and chips. But it had been *real*, Alexa. It was how it *would* be, I'm sure. When I'm ready; when HE's ready. When it happens – our great love.

Love

Gillian Freeborn

23 *Tudor Avenue*
Benbridge
Trowton TR0 9AF

Ms Alexa Deerheart   28 April
THE BIZZ

Dear Alexa

Thanks for your letter re Dad. You could be right, it *could* be a flash in the pan – a sort of momentary middle age panic. He did seem a bit depressed when he hit forty this year. He kept saying, 'Oh, my God, that's it now.' I'll just have to hold my breath and hope. . . .

Yesterday Rosalee floated downstairs in another creation from ZAP. A shimmery shiny slinky pale pink dress with a big V cut out of the back. I felt sick. She looked lovely. It didn't seem fair that someone so, well, horrible, could look so nice. She saw me staring at her, I couldn't help it, and she started swinging her hips and flicking her hair and pulling what she thought were the knowing, sophisticated expressions of a sensuous adult person.

'Wow!' said Dad, now a man of few syllables.

'Rosie,' said Mum. 'Not *another* new dress. It is lovely, but are you sure you can afford it, really? Are you sure you're not overcommitting yourself?'

''course not!' snorted Rosalee, as if she was above criticism. As if the cultivation of Rosalee Freeborn's wardrobe was a cause of such international importance that almost anything was justified.

She sat by the window, pulling at her hair and buffing up her nails, waiting for Sportsbag's crepe soles to crunch the gravel. And she waited and waited and waited while we all pretended not to notice that she'd started drooping and that a tear was trying to eject itself out of the corner of her eye. But the clock kept on ticking and soon it was nine o'clock and Rosalee was going red in the face and picking at the hem of her new pink dress.

Then she stood up and tore up the stairs two at a time, while Mum and Dad and me looked at each other with the unspoken words 'Greg's stood her up' sitting between us like an uninvited guest on the sofa. And, Alexa, it was ever so funny because even though Rosalee's the bane of my life, even though her every spare moment is spent in the relentless pursuit of the humiliation of her younger, more sensitive and creative sister, I felt sorry for her, and cross. I felt slighted too! I thought, How dare he, rotten sod.

Then all of a sudden Rosie shouted, 'Gilly! Come up here!' in this furious, ear-blasting voice.

She was standing in front of her mirror,

wiping rivers of mascara off her cheeks and taking deep breaths.

'Gill,' she said. 'Wanna come to Tricks with me? I'll ask Mum. You can wear my pink top if you like. It'll look nice with your blue skirt.'

Just like that. I nearly fell off my feet with surprise. But of course she didn't want to waste two hours' effort. Two hours spent soaking in the bath in Silky Soft Deep Penetrating Essence of Wild Rose Bath Oil, and applying face packs and face creams and face powder and spot camouflagers and cheek blusher and eye shadow and mascara and eyebrow pencil and all that stuff. And Mum said OK, as long as Dad took us there and picked us up at eleven o'clock. In fact she seemed rather pleased – she probably thought it was the beginning of the blossoming of deep and meaningful sisterly confidence. Oh, the easily deceived!

Rosalee was in such a hurry I barely had time to change into my blue skirt and throw on the pink top before we were in the car and on the way. I was feeling pretty bedraggled, and I suppose Rosalee felt sorry for me (or else she didn't want to look as if she hung around with spotty prepubescents) because she whipped out her make-up bag, said, 'Look at me a minute,' and did some quick, expert flicks on my face with brushes and pencils. Then she brushed back my hair from my face and pinned it with her favourite diamante clip!

'You look really good, Gill,' she said, examining her handiwork. And for a minute, Alexa, even *I* thought that maybe, perhaps, Rosalee really was changing, beginning to see me as more than a blight on the landscape of her life.

Didn't last long, though. I expect you can guess what happened. Rosalee *stormed* into Tricks, her eyes blazing, scanning the dance floor like lasers in search of the traitorous Greg. Of course, he wasn't there. So after getting us drinks and spending about five minutes pretending to make conversation with me, she got up to dance with a tall boy in a green fleece jacket called Cliff and hardly came back to the table all evening. No one asked me to dance, of course. I felt stupid just sitting there, the ugly sister, while Cinderella alternatively pranced and smooched to every record. I sat in the loo for half an hour, then spent a lot of time wandering around with half a glass of orange juice in my hand trying to look as if I was grooving to the music in a relaxed, disinterested sort of way, while really I was thinking that even the appearance of dribbling Wayne would be like a gift from heaven, which just shows you how low down and desperate I felt.

About ten to eleven, Rosalee came bounding up to me, grinning all over her face. 'Isn't he GORGEOUS!' she whispered breathlessly, grabbing hold of my arm and simpering in the direction of the men's loo where Cliff's green fleecy back could be seen disappearing. 'He's asked me out,' she went on, oblivious of my haughty disdain. 'Listen, I don't want him to know Dad's picking us up. I've said I've got to take you home, so go and wait outside and stop Dad coming in. I'll be out in a minute.'

Alexa, really! Dad was outside already, parked right in front of the door. As I got in the car, half of me wanted to rush back and interrupt Rosalee's snogging session with 'Daddy's waiting for us', but that was just the sort of thing *she'd* do and I wasn't going to sink to her level. Anyway, she came floating out two minutes later, all swaggery and triumphant, and flung herself into the car with a big satisfied sigh.

She tried to be all chatty and friendly on the way home, going on and on about Cliff this and Cliff that and how she didn't know what she had *ever seen* in Greg and, God, what a creep he was and how Cliff was a member of the Trowton Tennis Club. Might have guessed he'd be another sportsbag, Alexa. And Dad said, 'Gilly, did you enjoy yourself?' looking at me through the mirror. And I should have said, 'Yeah, I really enjoyed being *used*, used as a stooge for Rosalee Freeborn's ego; enjoyed being *ignored* by the entire youth of Trowton; enjoyed sitting in a toilet reading stimulating slogans like "Caz loves Baz" and "Fat Jo does it standing up"; enjoyed being a gullible *fool*.' That's what I *should* have said. But I said nothing, nothing at all. I just let myself collapse back in the seat, and sulked. I couldn't help it.

I suppose Rosalee must have been feeling a bit guilty because next morning at breakfast she was quite nice to me for about ten minutes before reverting to her usual vile invective. Well, I'd served my purpose, hadn't I. She didn't need me any more. I've had it with her, Alexa. That's the last time I'll ever be taken in. From now on it's every woman for herself. That's what I say.

Yours, an enlightened

Gilly Freeborn

23 *Tudor Avenue*
Benbridge
Trowton TR0 9AF

Ms Alexa Deerheart   30 April
THE BIZZ

Dear Alexa

Really, this is the last straw! Just as I'm beginning to feel that I've got a bit of cool; that I'm
not a 'ghastly nouveau-posh child of mindless
suburbia' to quote you-know-who, we've gone
and got a CLEANER! Ugh, how crass can you
get? Now we haven't only got our green luxury
shag pile carpet and crystal-drop mini chandelier, we've got someone to *clean* them. Mrs
Philipson is coming twice a week to clean up
after us and it makes me feel pretty low, I can
tell you. Mum is thrilled about it and keeps
saying, 'the cleaner' this, and 'the cleaner' that,
as if she were some sort of *thing* instead of a
person. I'm keeping pretty quiet about it – my
name'll be mud with Sarryan and Em if they
find out. On top of this, I don't really want a
complete stranger rummaging about in my
room, organizing my things into piles, digging
into my stack of *Bizz* mags and discovering
heaven knows what! My poems, for instance,
or your letters. So I told Mum that I didn't
want Mrs Philipson to do my room and that

I'd do it myself. And Mum said, That'll be the day, when the sky falls and fishes fly (which I thought was quite poetic for her).

So I've hidden my mags in the bottom of my wardrobe along with other personal and private stuff for my eyes only. She'd better not start nosing around, or there'll be *big* trouble, I can tell you!

Yours in disgust

Gillian Freeborn

23 Tudor Avenue
Benbridge
Trowton TR0 9AF

Ms Alexa Deerheart   3 May
THE BIZZ

Dear Alexa

Rosalee is sick in the mind. Depraved.

I changed my mind and decided that I would make an effort to develop a normal, loving, sisterly relationship, so on Sunday morning, I went into her room and sat on her bed in a friendly, confiding manner.

'What d'you think you're doing,' were her welcoming words. 'Get off my bed, creep!'

'Sorry,' I said, wounded. 'I only wanted to talk.'

'Well, I can't imagine you've got anything to say that will be of the remotest interest *to me*,' she replied, sitting at her dressing table and applying Country Cottage Biogenetic Primrose Cream to her face with vigorous strokes, all the time fluttering her eyelids in what she supposed was a sexy, sophisticated manner.

I decided that the only way to get through to her was to confide something deeply personal – something only a sister would understand. For a moment, I wondered about telling her about

102

HIM. Heaven knows, it would be a relief to confide in *someone*. But I thought better of it and said, 'I think I'm getting growing pains. Just here – a sort of achy, stretchy pain that comes and goes.'

''sprobably just your puppy fat relocating itself!' she guffawed. 'And get off my bed. Anyway, you're on Dad's side of the family so you'll most likely just have pimples like Auntie Paula – you'll be a fat little spotty creep with stubby legs and pimples. And anyhow, you're too retarded to have growing pains.'

'Well, Sarryan says– '

'Oh, *her*,' said Rosalee in this absolutely horrible sneery voice. 'We all know about *her*, putting it about everywhere.'

'Don't tell lies,' I said. 'Sarryan's great.'

'Yeah, that's what I've heard. I should think Michael Barnes thinks she's great, too. I've heard she was seen giving him a blow job in one of the changing rooms in the swimming pool.'

'What do you mean?'

'My God! Are you really that retarded? Don't you know *anything*? Haven't you ever heard of *oral sex*?' Then she shut the door and told me the most indescribably revolting thing that is too disgusting to write down on a respectable piece of paper.

'And then they EAT IT!' she finished with a final flick of her hair. Well, then I knew she was lying. I've heard some pretty ridiculous things in my life, but this took the biscuit. I called her a bloody liar and said that as she knew so much about it she must do it herself, trying to catch her out. 'Oh, *no*,' she said. 'It's only tarts who do it, and married people, because married people are allowed to do anything they like, and married people do it all the time – in fact they are probably doing it all over the country at this very moment!' And she said that I'd better get used to the idea because when I was married I'd have to do it too, whether I liked it or not. That is if I ever found anyone who didn't mind being married to a stubby-legged retard with pimples.

As you can imagine, Alexa, that just about finished me off. I didn't have much to say after *that* outburst. I think Rosalee must *really* hate me. Even if she's still annoyed about the Greg episode, which is fair enough, this was going too far, and anyway I haven't got stubby legs.

Do you know what I'm talking about, Alexa? It can't be true, can it? Sarryan wouldn't do it, I'm sure of that. I've known her since the infants.

I was mulling it over while I queued up at the corner shop next morning on the way to school. Mrs Bennet stood behind the counter in her blue nylon overall and funny, frizzy blue-rinsed hair and as I was buying a packet of M& Ms I suddenly got this vision of her on her knees grappling away at Mr Bennet's trousers in a frenzy. And then Mr Bennet himself emerged from behind a stack of Bounty Bar cartons with his completely bald head and his stomach bursting out of his shirt and I thought, NO! No way! There are just some things beyond anything and this is one of them. Apart from anything else, I just can't see the *point* of it.

Alexa, reassure me, please. I'm quite willing to accept the facts of life now, the basics. But tell me this other thing is something Rosalee has picked up from some pornographic magazine she's come across. *Normal* people don't do it, even if they're married, do they?

Yours in total perplexion

Gilly Freeborn

23 *Tudor Avenue*
Benbridge
Trowton TR0 9AF

Ms Alexa Deerheart   6 May
THE BIZZ

Dear Alexa

Well, blow me down! I'd never have believed it in a million years. Thanks for the booklet but quite frankly I've hardly had the heart to look at it. I know it's no good 'burying my head in the sand'. But 'all these things will seem pefectly natural when you're more mature and ready for a serious relationship' I just can't accept. I can't think of anything that will be less 'perfectly natural' to me even if I live to be 103. Yuk! I'm slowly coming to the conclusion that being grown-up is going to be a continuous round of emotional and physical torture. No wonder people get anorexia to try to stave it off. Angst-ridden adolescence seems tame in comparison. And it was no comfort when you said, 'Nobody will force you to do anything you don't want to do.' I mean, what if I get a husband who *insists* on it, every night? What if it's his favourite thing? What about *that*, eh? I feel sick at the thought.

Alexa, do you think there's something wrong with me? Do you think I ought to be getting *urges* to do these things? Do you think I really am naive and sexually retarded in some way? It's all so confusing.

Yours in disgust

Gilly Freeborn

23 *Tudor Avenue*
Benbridge
Trowton TR0 9AF

Ms Alexa Deerheart   9 May
THE BIZZ

Dear Alexa

I'm going off food. I've never been keen on meat, but now anything vaguely animal-like makes me feel like puking up, *especially* chicken. Last Sunday, Mum slapped this chicken *corpse* on the bread board and started *pulling it apart*. It was all goosepimply, like my legs when the bath water has gone cold. It was all bones and little limbs and stringy bits of veins and blobs. And Mum was just *dismembering* this once living member of the bird kingdom as if she had no more heart than Jack the Ripper.

'I'm not eating *that*,' I said. 'I'll just have vegetables.' And even though I said it quite calmly and politely, Mum went berserk and started going on and on about good food and slaving away in the kitchen and how many of my friends have Chicken Marengo carefully prepared for Sunday lunch – they were probably all force fed on a continuous diet of egg and chips. 'Well, what's wrong with egg and chips?' I said. 'I *love* egg and chips. Egg and chips is my favourite food.' I don't know why she's always insulting my friends as if our family was some kind of paragon institution that no other could possibly live up to. And then Mum just *yanked* this poor dead thing's leg off and I thought I was going to throw up there and then, right over the chicken corpse. That would have done it!

So, I had to sit through Sunday lunch forcing this dead flesh down my throat which kept threatening to come up again. And Dad was laughing at me, *laughing*! I thought at least *he'd* understand, but it seems that no one in our house is allowed to have principles or ideals 'cept for him. The result of all this is that I think I'm going to become a vegetarian, like Auntie Paula – although I may have the odd hamburger now and then, perhaps.

My favourite food:

EGG AND CHIPS!!!
Pizza
Crisps and cheese biscuits
Crispy stuffed pancakes
Any meat that doesn't look like meat, e.g. hamburgers, sausages, Spaghetti Bolognaise, etc.
hamburgers, sausages, mincemeat, etc.

Alexa, really, I think I'm old enough now to make decisions about what I eat. They can hardly stop me becoming a vegetarian, can they? I mean, it's not illegal, is it?

Yours rebelliously

Gilly Freeborn

PS   It had to happen! No one, not even the slim and beautiful, is immune from the invisible spores that float the air looking for a ripe young skin to set up home. What I'm trying to say is that Judy Fry has got a spot! A big spot, one of those pusy shiny ones, right on the end of her nose. It doesn't even look squeezable. It's gross – it may even be a *wart*. She has been walking around with her hand over her face because she can't bear to be seen as anything less than a flawless beauty. I'm afraid that's life, though, isn't it, Alexa?

23 *Tudor Avenue*
Benbridge
Trowton TR0 9AF

Ms Alexa Deerheart   13 May
THE BIZZ

Dear Alexa

Four rotten Saturdays! Four rotten Saturdays of greasy heads (really, I never knew people's heads could be so revolting – the balding ones with freckles are the worst, how they've got the nerve to come to a hairdresser in the first place, I don't know, exposing their flaking domes to complete strangers without a blink). Sweeping dead hair up off the floor is not something that comes naturally to me either, I can tell you. And if that isn't bad enough, I have to put up with *Zandra* (spotty, green dungarees) who thinks that just because she's one step up from me (she gets to 'comb out' – big deal!) she can boss me around as if I'm her own personal slave. 'Gilly, could you just pass me the oil of coconut. No, not *that* one, the *coconut* – you've got to learn,' and 'Gilly, you haven't swept under there. *Look*, you've missed a bit.' So I spend my whole time trying to annoy her by making sure I'm doing something for one of the stylists when I see her looking for some grot job to land me with. Really!

111

Every time the door opens I get this sort of twinge. It could be HIM. I never turn round *straight* away; I like to savour the anticipation, the possibility. But it never is. In four hair-sodden weeks, not a glimpse. But I've gone too far to pack it in now. I haven't gone through this *humiliation* for nothing. I'm keeping a close watch on his hair. It's creeping below his collar, little wisps are curling themselves round his ears. One day soon he'll come walking in for his cut and blow dry. I'll be ready.

Yours with fingers crossed

Gilly Freeborn

Ms Alexa Deerheart   15 May
THE BIZZ

Dear Alexa

I've hardly the heart to report my latest news.
Everything has been eclipsed by this terrible
row we've had at home. It was Sunday lunchtime and we were sitting at our reproduction
Louis XV mahogany veneer table shined to
mirror-like perfection and protected in force
by a battalion of 'Picturesque Ports of the
British Isles' place mats. I was starving, Mum
was starving, Rosalee was starving, but no
one was saying anything because Mum was
looking so terrifyingly *furious*. She kept staring
at the clock saying, 'Right,' every time the
minute hand clicked round.

Then about half-past two, the doorbell
rang. Mum rushed at it like a hundred metre
finalist in a rerun. But it was only Auntie Paula,
who sort of fell into the hall dropping her guitar
case on Mum's foot. 'Oh, God, it's you, Paula.
That's all I need!' Auntie Paula looked a little
hurt, not surprisingly, and said, 'Nice
welcome! Why are you so uptight, Michelle?'
which is the sort of thing guaranteed to turn

Mum into a raving maniac, if she isn't one already.

But Auntie Paula doesn't seem to notice atmospheres, bad ones anyway, and she swept into the dining room calling us Gillykins and Rosyposy and kissing us and dropping her bags and bits and pieces all over the floor. Then she sniffed at our gently burning roast and said, 'Oh, no, roast lamb! Goodness, I don't know how you can eat the dear little things. . . . I mean, when you see them frolicking around with their mums in the fields. Really, I don't know how you *can*!' which is the second sort of thing guaranteed to send Mum round the pole and back again.

And it was just at this moment, with Mum arguing about how she was trying to feed a family of growing girls a balanced diet and that Paula had no right to come into her house, etc. . . . when the key went in the lock and Dad suddenly burst into the middle of us all with his shirt buttons coming undone and singing 'I want to be FRE-EEEEE' in this incredibly loud and out-of-tune voice. And he was pretending to play the guitar and trying to cuddle Mum at the same time, which was like trying to cuddle an anaconda with toothache.

'For God's sake!' yelled Mum. 'Grow up. It's a quarter to three and if you think I've got nothing better to do than to hang around here waiting for a great lump of a drunken oaf who still thinks he's seventeen to come rolling in you've got another think coming.'

But Dad just reeled about bumping into Auntie Paula's bags saying, 'Oh, God, I feel sick,' and going green and yellow and white all at the same time.

'Quick, off my carpet!' screamed Mum.

And there followed this absolutely ear-scrunching row where Dad was saying, What did we want with a stupid pale green supersoft luxury shag pile for anyway just like all the other useless tasteless crap in this useless taste-less house and that it was all a horrible legacy of born-again Conservatism and what had hap-pened to all their IDEALS and how she had tricked him into believing she was someone she wasn't and how did she think he felt working all hours of the night and day like an automaton on a bloody INHUMAN computer to write programs so that lots of other greedy stupid people could buy their mock period houses and live on philistine estates like Benbridge, and on and on and on. And Mum *screamed* how she worked all hours too to make a lovely home and he'd be the first to complain if we didn't have it. . . .

And the three of us just stood there like mesmerized spiders and all the time I was thinking that these two fierce and furious war-riors had actually *done it,* from choice.

Then Dad went upstairs and fell asleep with all his clothes on. And Mum suddenly went all quiet and stiff and told us to sit down, and Auntie Paula too. Then she started preparing lunch, picking everything up really carefully and slowly and precisely, as if she were performing brain surgery. And as she was serving up she began crying in this funny sort of sniffly way and great big tear drops were dropping into the mint sauce and I started thinking that Dad was a bastard, even though I agreed with him about the green luxury shag pile which had been the bane of my life since I was about ten years old.

Mum sat with us, although she only ate about half a Brussels sprout. I ate everything on my plate, even the tear-flavoured mint sauce, and said it was lovely.

The afternoon just sort of died. Rosalee, Auntie Paula and I did the washing-up. Then Rosalee went round to her friend Tamsin's house for a mutual blackhead-squeezing session. Auntie Paula just picked up all her bags and went back to London without saying anything at all.

I sat in this awful silence punctuated only by Dad's bone-shaking snores. I decided to go for a walk. Alexa, I think I'm going off love. Do you think Mum ever felt the same way about Dad as I feel about HIM? Do you think my parents are cracking up? Do you think I'll ever turn into a born-again Conservative with a tasteless house? Do you think HE'll ever fall

in love with me? What will happen? Let me
know what you think.

Yours on a gloomy Monday evening on
Benbridge Estate.

Best wishes

Gilly Freeborn

23 Tudor Avenue
Benbridge
Trowton TR0 9AF

Ms Alexa Deerheart   19 May
THE BIZZ

Dear Alexa

OK. But how do you know? How can you be so sure of yourself? When I read your column, it all sounds as if absolutely *everything* is going to turn out all right for absolutely *everyone*. But how *can* it? I mean, what would you say if I told you, 'Mum 'n' Dad have split up for ever. They're getting divorced and they're putting me in a children's home run by depraved sadistic child torturers.' What would you say to that, eh? Probably, 'Well, never mind. These things happen; lots of kids go through the same experience and are able to live perfectly normal and happy lives!' I bet that's what you'd say.

Still, I suppose you get about a million-zillion letters a week and have a hard time keeping up. So, OK, you've got to give answers, but they're not *real*, are they? Maybe you've even got a special computer program capable of dealing with every potential teenage problem, like, for instance:

A-BREASTS

1. Too big   2. Droopy

3. Too small   4. Too high

5. Nonexistent   6. Too low

7. Hairy nipples   8. The unexplainable

And you press Option 8, for instance, and out comes your standard letter. You just fill in the relevant details:

Dear Worried Sick of Basildon

Please don't worry that your bosoms are **growing ginger hair and sprouting warts and hanging down to your knees**. No one really cares about these things. Bodies come in all shapes and sizes. You'd be surprised at the quite trivial things that people worry about. It's all part of growing up.

Why not just be honest:

Dear Overweight Monster from Potters Bar

God, you sound hideous! What rotten luck. It must be bloody awful to be four foot one and fifteen stone. I can't imagine what it must be like to heave that great wobbling mass of flab around. I'd emigrate to Outer Mongolia, if I were you.

or

I was sorry to hear about your penis. It does sound *incredibly* small. It must be hell in the changing room, as you say, especially now the green mange has taken hold. My advice to you is to keep it under wraps at all costs. Don't let anyone get even a hint of it, or your name'll be mud.

You see! At least it's straightforward and honest!

So you think everything will be all right with Mum and Dad, do you? If I just 'keep relaxed and be supportive. Most marriages have their ups and downs.' Well, Alexa, I hope you're right, though things look pretty bleak at the moment. Mum's taken to spending *hours* talking to her friend Jackie on the upstairs phone. And when Mum got dressed up to go to cocktails at Dr Price's, Dad just flopped on the sofa and refused to go saying he didn't want to waste a perfectly good evening standing round with a load of Bupa cardholders drinking so-called 'sparkling wine' and eating 'gnat food' and that he was going to the New Green Man for some decent grub like shepherd's pie and chips. And Mum said, 'OK, if you want to behave like the great uncouth slob you are, you'll show yourself up. You won't need me to do it.' And she went on her own. I heard all this while plucking my eyebrows in the downstairs loo.

Well, whether or not it's going to 'turn out

all right' I'm not going to take any chances. I'm going to see if I can't help them on the way to rediscovering those first intense passionate love feelings they must have had when they met. I'm going to find out the favourite songs of their youth and play them nonstop. Sarryan's dad's got a 'Greatest Hits of the Sixties' tape. At least it's worth a try, eh? Better than doing nothing.

You see, there're only a few weeks to go till the summer holidays. We're supposed to be going to a hotel in Majorca with an enormous swimming pool with a water chute. I mean, you can't take any chances, can you?

Yours

Gilly Freeborn

23 Tudor Avenue
Benbridge
Trowton TR0 9AF

Ms Alexa Deerheart   23 May
THE BIZZ

Dear Alexa

Sorry again. Of course I don't really think you're a computer. I just got sort of fed up and frustrated. I mean, things are much more complicated than you can say in a letter, aren't they? There are the *nuances*, the things that sort of float around in the air without anyone putting words to them. I know you have to be positive, to keep people's spirits up, look on the bright side. Only sometimes, nothing anyone says makes you feel all right. Things have either happened or they haven't and you either feel this or that about them. Do you know what I mean?

At least I've got my poems, though. They're sort of keeping me going at the moment, especially as I seem to have reached even further heights of invisibility and insignificance as far as HE is concerned. I'm getting really worried that he's *growing* his hair and that I'm wasting the best Saturdays of my young life slaving away in that rotten shop with Giorgio prancing around massaging people's egos by

telling them stuff like 'youa looka *bellissima* dar-
linga,' or 'youa gonna knockam deada wid zat
new colour.' And *Zandra*, spot face, every week
puffing up bigger and bigger with self-import-
ance, like some great slimy spotted toad.

We went to Bournemouth on Sunday to visit
Grandma Freeborn and to give Rosalee a
chance to exhibit herself in her new pink Lycra
bikini. It was too cold to go in so I lay on the
sand in my T-shirt, letting the waves trickle
over my toes. Then all of a sudden the sky
turned black with smoke. The plane was down.
Our section had broken away and we were
floating loose in the wild sea, the waves beating
against our fragile craft. I sat there, frozen,
trance-like, still strapped in, unable to move.
'Come, *darling*,' HE beseeched, frantically
undoing my seat belt and taking off my dress,
pausing for a moment to gaze with astonishment on the loveliness of my slender frame.
'Oh, you gorgeous thing,' he says. 'I'll save you.
But quick, *quick*. The sharks are gathering.'
That did it. I bravely leapt into the murky deep,
and together we swam and swam. Ahead was
an island, its silky sand glistening in the distance. Its palm fronds waving. I was exhausted,
but on and on I swam, love fuelling my
strength, till I collapsed, faint on the shore.
    Strong brown naked arms are round me,
lifting my feather-light frame from the clutches

of the sea. But HE is wounded. A great gash slashed across his thigh. He starts to crumble; I pick him up. Super-human strength sears through my bones. I carry him to the shade of a palm tree. His eyes are closed. 'Don't die! Don't die! Darling,' I cry, anguished. For two days and nights I tend his precious torso, oblivious to the dark dangers that lurk in that mysterious domain. I clean his wound, wash his face, cool him with my loving breath. On the third morning, his eyelids flutter. He opens his eyes, his deep brown eyes intense, resplendent under lustrous lashes.

'Oh, my *love*,' he cries. 'Can this happiness be true? Fate and Faith have kept us both alive to be together, always.' We rise and explore the island. Luscious fruits hang from the trees. We shake down some coconuts and drink our fill. 'We will live here forever, my darling,' he says, 'away from the cruelness of the world. How I ever thought I loved that stringy beanbag with her ghastly spot, I shall never know.'

We run into the sea. Our bodies touch. Our lips. . . . Alexa, I'm getting spasms writing this. I think I should stop. The truth is, Mum burst right into this bliss-filled reverie with, 'Put some of this insect repellent on, Gilly. The midges are biting. You know what you're like with your skin.'

And I was back in my own body. Round and red. A rash on my stomach where I'd been lying on the sand. A dead fly squashed against my leg. Such are the cruel realities of life.

Hope to have some real news to report soon.

Love

Gilly Freeborn

Ms Alexa Deerheart   26 May
THE BIZZ

Dear Alexa

Pennings is a hypocritical creep. A lizard. Well,
what could you expect, really. He's a man, the
worst sort. One that says one thing and believes
another. Any man over twenty is the same.
They've been pampered and coddled by
women and never had to lift a finger to look
after themselves. We know whose side *they're*
on.

 Sarry and I went to confront him about our
demands, but he just went all sort of false
and friendly and patronizing, saying, 'Yes, girls,
these are all good points, perfectly logical and
in an *ideal* world' – and here he leaned across
his desk with a really stupid between-you-and-
me look – 'it would of course all be possible.
And if it were up to me . . .' etc., etc. 'But we
do have the Education Authority to contend
with, and with quite *major* changes like this the
organization, the *administration* is just mind-
boggling. But I'm sure all these things are
under review, changes *are* happening behind
the scenes, although maybe not as fast as we

would all like. I'm sure you understand. Anyway, girls, I think we can act independently on one or two of these points, don't you,' – pathetic wink – 'I've told Mrs Brown that the boys are to help with the Open Day buffet, serving and things. And I've suggested to Mr Creswell that if there *are* any girls interested in football or rugby, he might think about starting up a special session after school. Well, what do you think of that!'

Sarryan gave me a fierce sideways look, as if to say, 'Go on then.'

'Well I'm afraid it's just not good enough, Mr Pennings,' I said. 'Not good enough. Don't you realize that Langley Street is *way* behind other schools, where these common human rights are taken for *granted*. Our members will not be happy with this, I can tell you.'

Well, really, Alexa. You know what he said? He said, 'Now, I'm very busy, girls. I've got to get on. I hope you're putting the same enthusiasm into your school work as you are into all this campaigning.' And he just got up and opened the door.

Well, I called an emergency LSHYWAC meeting that evening and reported his pathetic response. Sarry was all for going on strike. But I had a better idea. We'd write to the newspapers! As a first step. We drafted up a letter, and Ranesh Japoor suggested that we show it to Mrs Goldstein. Get her involved. After all, she is a woman.

Annie and Brainbox didn't even come. It just goes to show you, doesn't it, that some people can let their personal feelings get in the way of more important, international concerns, like basic human rights. I only hope that HE reads the Trowton *Evening Echo*. It's half-term next week. I'll keep you informed.

Yours

Gilly Freeborn

23 Tudor Avenue
Benbridge
Trowton TR0 9AF

Ms Alexa Deerheart   31 May
THE BIZZ

Dear Alexa

> *Love caught my breath*
> *When I gazed upon*
> *His lovely face.*
> *It took my voice:*
> *The very hymn I sung*
> *Was stolen for*
> *His own.*
> *But, oh!*
> *No answering song*
> *Echoed.*

Waddayathink? Coming on? I know it's not perfect, but I do feel I'm getting somewhere. I feel I'm expressing *some* of my inner turmoil.

Sometimes, Alexa, I can't sleep. I lie awake for *hours*, listening to the buzz of distant traffic, listening to Mum and Dad arguing in undertones in bed, listening for Rosalee's footsteps to come click-clicking down the road. And when all the noise stops I sometimes feel *terrified*, as if the whole world is dead and I'm the only one alive, lying in my house in my room

129

in Benbridge Estate. I get this sort of ringing in my ears and I hardly dare *move* in case the whole thing comes tumbling down on me. Do you know what I mean? So it's then that I make up the poems in my head (they sort of lull me off to sleep). And I try to remember them in the morning, but they're never as good though. I thought of a *really* good one last night but when I woke up I could only remember the last line: '*And his passion was fire-red, like rocket flames burning the night sky bright . . .*' then, nothing! I'll have to keep a pen and paper by my bed.

And because I've been so tired, I've been bad-tempered and snappy, like some sort of crotchety crocodile. Snap! Snap! Dad keeps telling me to 'cheer myself up' and Mum keeps trying to force me to eat steak and chicken and stuff in the mistaken belief that meat is some kind of miracle food without which no teenager can possibly reach full adult-hood and still be healthy in body and mind. Then because she's not getting anywhere, she's begun *disguising* it. 'Here's a nice crunchy salad,' she says, and I'll find this huge hunk of chicken armed with a lethal piece of *gristle* lying in ambush among the lettuce. I'm not daft, Alexa, whatever people might think.

I know they all think I'm lazy and stupid; they think I should be out there swimming and playing tennis and whooping it up in the fresh air, getting rid of all that excess energy that teenagers are supposed to have. But I haven't got any excess energy. I've hardly got enough *ordinary* energy to move my bones through the day. I feel just like a great lump of adolescent flesh, heaving itself about, sloth-like and moribund. And *still* no breasts! The so-called 'growing pains' are manifesting themselves now and again, but on the material front – nothing! If I throw my shoulders forward, I can sometimes deceive myself that there's some sort of matter there, but I'm not convinced. And if you can't fool yourself, who can you fool? Oh, *how* long before the natural development, the maturing of the human body, which happens to every single person in the world, starts happening to me? I feel angst-ridden.

Yours, a fed-up

Gilly Freeborn

23 Tudor Avenue
Benbridge
Trowton TR0 9AF

Ms Alexa Deerheart   4 June
THE BIZZ

Dear Alexa

I don't think I've ever been close to murder, not really. Zandra, *Zandra*! How that name evokes visions of lizards and slime toads and scaly creeping creatures whose little beady eyes swivel around on sticks and whose undersized brains are diminishing at the rate of about two million cells an hour, wearing themselves out thinking up schemes to make life as miserable and low down menial as possible for other more intelligent and creative people.

It was a scorcher of a day again. My nylon overall was torture, sucking at my skin like a spacesuit with a puncture. I kept having to stand under the fan to dry off my fringe which was sending little rivers down my forehead to drip off the end of my nose and on to people's domes. And all the time *Zandra* was watching me out of the corner of her eye, sort of *twitching* as if she had something on her tiny mind (she certainly did, as I found out later)! I wasn't allowed to stand still for a second without her sickening whine invading my eardrums with

132

'G-i-l-l-y! When you've *finally* done that could you please fetch some more oil of coconut from the cupboard/sweep up that hair/tidy up the reception desk/answer the phone/*wipe the conditioner bottles*,' – would you believe it! She wasn't happy unless I had at least six pathetic futile tasks lined up one after the other.

If I'd had even an *ounce* of nous about me that morning I'd have sussed the situation; I'd have read the vibes and could have worked out some sort of *counter plan*. But I had no idea that imbeciles could be so *devious*.

'O'Neil. Cut and blow dry.' Just like that! I was in the middle of shampooing Mrs (Pork Chop) Parkinson when these longed-for words came drifting through the whir of hairdryers and the slosh-slurp of showers and landed in my eardrums, sending spasms from the top of my head to my toes. It had happened.

But before I even had time to *breathe*, a flash of green dungaree *streaked* across the floor and hurled itself behind the reception desk. I felt this sick sort of panic well up in my chest, and it caught hold of a fierce anger at the sudden realization that lizard-features had looked at the appointment book and had probably been scanning its pages every single Saturday. That was why she'd been gyrating about all morning like a ping-pong ball with delirium shakes.

And then the panic and anger joined forces with a sort of self-loathing at my stupidity for not doing the same thing until I was positively *charged* with venom and capable of the most extreme action the circumstances could offer. So, without thinking, I poured the whole bottle of 'Primrose Cream Shampoo for dry, brittle and heat-damaged hair' all over Mrs Parkinson's Brillo-pad perm and began massaging like mad. In a second she had a four-foot tower of shampoo, throbbing and oozing and growing bigger by the second.

'ZANDRA!' I screamed. 'There's something wrong with this shampoo. Quick, Look! It's gone mad.'

And Zandra, who was lovingly draping HIM with towels in preparation for his shampoo, was forced to come over to my basin while I affected a look of puzzled astonishment as the foamy monster seethed heavenwards.

'What'n earth have you done, stupid!' she screeched. 'You've put far too much on!'

'No I haven't!' I cried indignantly. 'There's something wrong with it. It must be a sort of mutant bottle that's got over-concentrated. I haven't got the experience to deal with something like this. I'll do your shampoo.'

So with Zandra red in the face with fury, because the more water she put on the bigger it grew, I, with these great lurching feelings in my chest, *leaned* over HIM and turned on the shower, my hand actually upon his silken locks.

134

And I was just about to *begin* when Giorgio ran across the room shouting, 'What goin' on here? Who doin' this foamy stuff!'

And by this time you could hardly even *see* Mrs Porkchop, she was like 'The Giant Fizz Ball That Fell to Earth' – a great oozing blob squeaking 'eek! eek!' And Reptile Face said, 'Oh, Mr Giorgio, it was *Gilly*. She did it *on purpose*! She used the *whole bottle*.' The low-down creep that she is. The *grub worm*. And Giorgio started shouting at me and everyone in the shop was staring and I was furious because I suddenly realized that all those tortuous Saturdays had come to nothing because I was going to get the sack and HE was sitting, exposed and vulnerable just two inches away, listening to me being *humiliated* by a cretinous embryonic *hairdresser* in green dungarees.

So I didn't give them a chance. I just said, as coolly as I could, 'I can't help it if the shampoo is faulty. And anyway, I've got better things to do with my time than pamper people's vanity. I'm a poet!' And I threw off my pink overall, picked up my bag and strode to the door just in time to hear HIM say, 'Hey, I think I *know* her,' which was like glorious fairy music to my ears. He had recognized me. My features are imprinted on his brain.

So that's the end of 'My Life as a Hair-dresser', thank God! At least I know I'm made for better things. I hope when Zandra reads about me in the newspapers, when she's slaving

135

away in some compression chamber called Susie's or Enrico's, she'll realize that I'm one and the same.

Really, though, Alexa, you can understand if I feel a bit down. My fantasy flopped, dismally. It was a complete bomb at the box office and this investor is badly out of pocket.

Still, every sow's ear has a silk purse inside somewhere, doesn't it? Plan B will be born. More about that soon.

Yours

Gilly Freeborn

PS   I'm glad you think my poems are coming on. I've written twenty-four now. My blue book is almost full.

23 Tudor Avenue
Benbridge
Trowton TR0 9AF

Ms Alexa Deerheart   7 June
THE BIZZ

Dear Alexa

Well, we typed up our letter. We showed it to
Mrs Goldstein and asked her if the teachers
would support us. She said she agreed with us
and even made a couple of suggestions, but
that it was difficult for individual teachers to
get involved in something like this. Really!
What has happened to moral fibre? Nothing
will ever be achieved if even people who believe
in things are more worried about themselves
than the cause. Sarryan said it made her feel
sick.

Anyway, Sarry, Em, Ranesh and I went
together to post the letter. We all signed it.
Even Phyllis managed a scribbly scrawl. Keep
your fingers crossed. Any day now our names
could appear in print! We'll show him he can't
patronize *us*!

Yours

Gilly Freeborn

23 *Tudor Avenue*
Benbridge
Trowton TR0 9AF

Ms Alexa Deerheart   16 June
THE BIZZ

Dear Alexa

What can I do? What can be *done*? There's a party a week tomorrow in London. I think I'm old enough to go. I mean, I am fourteen and pretty sensible and anyway I can't see why I shouldn't be considered capable of getting on a train and coming back again without becoming a heroin addict or being raped and ruined by sex-starved perverts on the way. Especially as I'll be with Sarryan and Em – they can hardly kidnap all three of us at the same time, can they?

It's Sarryan's sister's eighteenth birthday and the party is on a *houseboat*. Judy's going, so you know what *that* means.

'Will your mum let you go?' said Sarryan on Monday.

'Dunno,' was my enigmatic response. Though in reality there's as much chance of that as there is of Judy Fry falling passionately in love with Wayne Cross. And Alexa, the more I think about it, the more angry I get. I mean, how come Sarry and Em are allowed to go to a party in London, when I'm hardly allowed to walk down the road without the dressing-table sentry watching my every step?

And all the way through rotten maths I was meditating on the miscarriage of justice, and I went into another trance with the words 'bloody hell, it's not fair' buzzing round and round my brain like a mantra. There's no harm in asking, I was thinking to myself, they can't *kill* me for asking. But then I thought, No, once they get wind of it they'll be watching me like hawks and Rosalee'll be saying, '*I* was never allowed to do anything like that at *her* age,' in her sneery voice. So I started making this plan, this Mum-proof scheme, where I could go to the party and get back home by half-past eleven by using Grandma Freeborn's birthday money for a taxi from the station.

And just as I had got it all figured out, Mr Parkins (Parrot Beak) broke into my reverie with, 'And the method is, *Gillian?*' and this horrendous equation on which we were supposed to be working materialized in front of my eyes, spreading across the page like a huge black spider. I went into a sort of paralysis at the sight of it. Then the bell rang and Parrot Beak told me to stay behind because he had 'something to say to me'. So I had to sit at my desk while everyone filed out giving me sympathetic looks, all except for Annie who stuck her head in the air as if to say, 'You're going down the academic drain, Gilly Free-born. Look what you've come to.'

Then Parkins made me come over to his desk and squawked on and on about 'not concentrating' and 'using what little brain cells you've got' and 'at least you used to make an effort' and 'it's all very well starting campaigns, but it's the plain hard work, the GCSEs that are going to count' and 'what on earth is going on in that head of yours?'

And all the time I was thinking, I'm going! I'm going! I'm going! I'm going to the party and I just don't care.

Yours

Gilly Freeborn

23 *Tudor Avenue*
Benbridge
Trowton TR0 9AF

Ms Alexa Deerheart   10 June
THE BIZZ

Dear Alexa

Saturday. Sarryan and I were sitting in the Fresh Bake drinking espressos. We were sitting in our favourite window seat gazing through the rubber plant leaves at the faces of passers-by. The café was full of Blobs. The whole of Trowton seems full of Blobs sometimes: round old ladies with curly perms, raincoats, plastic shoes and shopping bags. 'Old bags' Sarryan calls them. And they're accompanied by the 'Fuds' – fuddy-duddy men in blue acrylic short-sleeved shirts with holes in them, and Crimplene trousers with shiny buttons. Blobs and Fuds, thousands of them, born out of square houses with aluminium window frames and nurtured on MFI sales and Bejams.

'God, I hope I don't look like *that* when I'm thirty!' snorted Sarryan, tilting her head towards a table full of wobblers that looked at least forty-five to me.

''course you won't,' I said. Somehow I couldn't imagine Sarryan at thirty, which seems ancient, nearly as old as my mum!

Sarry looked fantastic again. I know her mum doesn't have much money, but Sarry always seems able to *improvise*. She was wearing a wide silver band round her hair and a shiny black short sleeveless dress she got from the cancer shop. Her nails were bright blue and her lips were neon pink. She looked sophisticated, grown up. Gloom. Suddenly, I realized that HE could never take me seriously. Not when I looked like a toddling blubbery seal with its baby fur still hanging off.

'Sarryan,' I said meaningfully. 'How old do you think I look?'

Sarryan put down her cup and looked at me for a long time. 'Well, Gilly,' she said. 'You look older when you're dressed up.'

'But how old do you think I look *now*, in this T-shirt, or in my school clothes?' I tried to affect a serious, mature look by tilting my head on the side and smiling a knowing smile.

'Well, to be honest, Gill, you look your age, I mean, fourteen. It doesn't help that you haven't got any boobs yet – though I'm sure you'll get them soon.'

Oh, flying armadillos! I knew. I knew it! Why is it that we have to ask questions that we don't want the answers to, eh? Like when Mum says, 'Do you think I'm putting on weight?' and Dad drops his newspaper and takes off his glasses and says, 'Oh, my God, I hadn't noticed, you're ENORMOUS! Like a great beached whale. Your *bottom*!'

And Mum says, deadly serious, 'What's *wrong* with my bottom? Don't be horrible. I've only put on a couple of pounds.'

And then they have a great blazing row, all because Dad told Mum what she knew in the first place. I can understand. You sort of hope that somehow the mirror has warped itself. That it's not giving you the true picture. That you're not seeing yourself as others see you.

'Cheer up, you,' said Sarryan. 'Tell you what. Come round early on Saturday and I'll do your make-up, properly. I bet I can make you look eighteen.'

And that's what we decided. Sarryan is going to make me up for the party, *and* she's going to hide Rosalee's big white linen jacket in her house so I can wear it on the night.

I'll let you know how things go.

Yours

Gilly Freeborn

23 *Tudor Avenue*
Benbridge
Trowton TR0 9AF

Ms Alexa Deerheart   19 June
THE BIZZ

Dear Alexa

I know it's wrong to lie, I *know.* But it's too late now. I don't suppose Sarry and Em will ever speak to me again. My own family is treating me like an untouchable, a degenerate, something that's lower than a maggot, a grub, a germ.

Well, I went. I told them I was going to Sarryan's to listen to cds. Which was true. Except that while the Eruptions rapped out *Big Rap Talking Blues Number Twelve* Sarry was doing her best to perform miracles with various creams, paints, powders and gels in the purpose of transforming a gawky fourteen-year-old into a sophisticated *femme fatale*. 'You look *great!*' said Sarryan when she'd finished. I wasn't sure. I had black lines around my eyes, scarlet cheeks and neon pink lipstick. I had this uneasy feeling that I looked more like a five-year-old who'd been to a face painting party than the trendy, stylish eighteen-year-old of my dreams. But there was no time to change my mind. I threw on Rosie's cream linen jacket and we rushed off to meet Em at the station.

It was while we were sitting on the train that the *enormity* of what I'd done suddenly hit me. It seemed like such a *big* lie. What if Mum phoned Sarry's and found I wasn't there, what if I got lost, what if I missed the last train, what if they called *the police*! And while Sarry and Em were rapping on about who would be there and who would be wearing what and all that stuff, my insides started going all queasy. I felt as if my intestines were *melting*, turning to green goo and slolloping about in my stomach, squishing around to the rhythm of the train. I began to wish I was back at home, lying on our Dralon stripe watching the final part of 'Dark Night' and eating egg and chips.

Sarry's sister's boyfriend met us off the train and drove us to the boat. I felt a bit better when we got to the party. There weren't too many people there at first. Sarry asked them to play the Eruptions and the three of us did the switch. We'd been practising and we did it really well. Everyone clapped and I began to relax a bit. It was a great place to have a party – there were fairy lights strung all round the deck and heaps of food and a lovely fruity drink with bits of orange and lemon floating around in it. But the biggest excitement was when HE arrived. You see, everybody turned to look at him, he was so beautiful. He was wearing dark blue combat trousers and a pale blue denim shirt. He floated down the steps, with Judy behind him sporting a beautiful blue silk dress with a slit, a black

145

jacket and *the spot*! It was obviously one of those *deep-rooted*, stubborn jobs, immune to Spot Off and Zit Blitz which the television tells us are the natural enemies of the teenage pimple. And when HE went off to fetch the drinks, we rushed up and told her she looked very nice and stuff but all she could talk about was her spot, as if it was impossible for her even to *exist* with a blemish, that she could hardly believe such a thing had the nerve to descend on *her*. 'I've tried *everything*,' she whimpered in nasal tones (she had her hand over her nose all the time she was speaking), 'but nothing works, it just gets *worse*.'

We got fed up with this whining self-pity and anyway HE was coming back and I didn't want to risk another vibe attack in full view of Judy. Michael Barnes turned up and Sarry did her usual disappearing act. So I dragged Em off to the buffet where I could examine him at a safe distance. I was digging into the prawn crackers, simultaneously watching HIS every move out of the corner of my eye when two boys came up and started talking to Em. They started asking her where she came from and who she knew and stuff, and *completely* ignored me, both of them. And then one of them said, 'Is that your little sister?' sort of nastily, which just about finished me off. So I just left Em there and picked up a glass of fruit juice. That was my downfall.

I guess that in my heart of hearts I *knew* it wasn't just fruit juice, Alexa. Because after the first glass I started to feel all bubbly and completely forgot about Mum and Dad and telling lies and getting home and stuff. It was hot, so hot. I was all sweaty and thirsty and fed up at always being the one who was left out. And I must have drunk two or three glasses, for the music started sounding really loud and the room started swimming all round. I didn't even like it. The next thing I remember is that even though someone was throwing gallons of cold water over me, I couldn't move. I was sort of *paralysed*. I thought I must be dying at the least. And then the words 'your parents are here' broke through the fuzzy, furry, woolliness of my brain which was already pounding with a hundredweight of headache. And what I didn't know was that I'd been sick all over my skirt and Em had *taken it off*. So Mum and Dad weren't at all pleased to see me carried up the plank, bottom first, with my Marks and Spencer red rose knickers glowing like a beacon and portending all sorts of ghastly horrors that they couldn't really be expected to believe hadn't happened. And Dad went *berserk* and screamed at Sarryan and Emily and called them 'a bad influence' and he was 'going to have a few words to say to their parents' and Mum was all for calling the police, but Em was in tears saying, 'but she was *sick*, honest. Nothing happened.' And it wasn't until Dad and Mum interrogated every single person at the party, including the bar staff and the waitresses, that they believed I hadn't been forcibly drugged and used in a wild sex orgy. My only consolation is that HE wasn't there to witness it. Judy had been unable to cope with her blemished nose and they had gone home early.

You see, Dad had phoned when I hadn't gone home by twelve and of course Sarry's mum told him where we were. Sarry got in a heap of trouble for lying about me being allowed to go. And I'm in a heap of really big trouble, Alexa. And I suppose you think I deserve it. Well, I do. It seems as though things'll never get back to normal. I doubt whether I'll ever be allowed out, ever again.

Yours in penitence

Gilly Freeborn (reformed)

PS This humiliating experience wasn't *entirely* wasted, though, Alexa. Lying in the back of the car, doubled up with nausea and feeling as if my guts were going to shoot up my windpipe and out of my mouth of their own accord, I was *compos mentis* enough to notice that Mum and Dad were actually *talking* to each other. Phrases like 'God, she's only fourteen' and 'How are we going to handle this' and 'It could've been worse' and stuff like that came drifting through my brain-fuzzed state. As I've said before, every sow's ear has a silk purse. Anyway, that's what I'm telling myself.

23 Tudor Avenue
Benbridge
Trowton TR0 9AF

Ms Alexa Deerheart   25 June
THE BIZZ

Dear Alexa

Things have calmed down a bit. I think they've
realized that I'm not really in danger of going
off the rails, of falling into shameful
degeneracy. Of course, Rosalee's been having
a field day, saying, 'You'll have to watch her
now. She can't be trusted,' and even, 'Cliff
thinks she shouldn't be allowed out at all until
she's fifteen,' as if it's got anything to do with
him.

I'd completely forgotten about the jacket,
so it was a bit of a shock when two days later
Rosalee dug inside a Sainsbury's plastic bag
and pulled out what looked like a scrunched
up table cloth after a particularly messy dinner
party. 'Oh, my GOD!' she squawked in tortured tones, staring up at the ceiling and
gyrating as if she were having some sort of fit.
'My jacket, my *jacket!*' Mum and Dad had to
restrain her as she lunged towards me, teeth
gnashing like a wild beast attacking its prey. I
honestly thought my time was up, Alexa.
Luckily Mum managed to calm her down by

149

saying I'd have to pay for it to be cleaned and that if the cleaning didn't work I'd have to *buy* her another one out of my birthday money. It's a miracle isn't it, Alexa, with the chemicals they've got nowadays they can clean almost *anything*, even blood. So a little bit of two-day-old congealed sick shouldn't be too much of a problem, should it?

I've been doing lots of washing-up and *homework* and sorting out my room and *ironing* and just being very, very quiet and unobtrusive. Wednesday evening I offered to help Dad in the garden, said I'd dig over the overgrown patch at the back. Dad said I'd do better to dig over my own conscience to see if I couldn't clear that up first. And I said, What did I have to *do* to prove to them that I was sorry and Dad said, 'Clean out the garage,' which is a job Mum has been going on about him doing for about twenty years. And he laughed, then I laughed, and I suppose things seemed on the way to being back to normal.

Sarry and Em have been all right. We even managed to laugh about it later. 'If you could have seen your dad's face,' said Sarry, 'when they carried you down the plank.' I suppose it was rather funny, really.

I had a lovely dream last night. I can't tell you exactly what happened but it started off with my swimming costume being too small. I woke up in a passionate clinch with my pillow.

The world of puberty is indeed a strange and puzzling one.

Love

Gilly

PS   Now everything's calmed down again, Mum and Dad are getting back into their you-snap-at-me-and-I'll-bite-your-head-off routine. On and on and on. . . . Where will it end?

Ms Alexa Deerheart   2 July
THE BIZZ

Dear Alexa

I'm feeling sick with myself. I'm becoming OBSESSED with my face. I don't seem capable of passing a mirror without staring at my chubby mug, examining it for potential eruptions or deformities. I keep telling myself that this is perfectly normal behaviour for a growing teenager – I mean, *anything* could happen with all those hormones multiplying themselves down there, sorting themselves into the different sections of the future Gilly Freeborn, the one who will be facing the world as a fully formed adult person.

But I've got this guilty feeling that I'm just VAIN, because what does it matter, really, when every day the world throws up some mind-shattering threat to the continuance of humanity, like nuclear accidents and droughts and famines and the poisoning of the *sea* (which throws up poor dead bloated seals and dolphins and stuff on the *beaches*) and of the *earth* (where chemical-reprocessing plants are causing children to be born with only one eye, or to die of leukaemia before they're even five years old and not even getting a chance to examine their faces in the mirror to worry about what they're going to look like when they're twenty-one). Then there're equal opportunity and unemployment and not enough money in the Health Service (which means according to Dad that more and more old people are going to start dropping dead in the street from hyperthermia and broken hips).

There're all these things, and more, but I just can't seem to stop this relentless examination even though it fills me with self-loathing. And you won't be surprised when you hear what I've discovered.

I was using my new two-mirror technique to examine places inaccessible by normal means when I discovered with revulsion that – my *nostrils* are TOO BIG! They're *enormous*, like great huge gaping hairy holes. Full frontal, my nose looks fairly normal, apart from a small bump in the middle which gives me a bit of character, I think. But from *underneath*, HORROR!

So later that evening I lay on the floor to try to get a look at Rosalee's breathers and they are about *half the size* of mine. I think I'm turning into a freak!

And there's worse. Saturday afternoon was baking hot. I was sitting on my bed looking out of the window in dreamy contemplation of *Wuthering Heights* when Rosalee came into the garden wearing her tiny pink Lycra bikini. She sort of floated across the lawn and lowered herself into our sunflower sun lounger, letting one slim leg dangle over the edge for effect. She has *tiny* ankles on the end of long thin legs and as I was staring at these delicate little ankles the meaning of 'Rosalee has inherited Grandpa Freeborn's bone structure' became patently and painfully clear. Grandpa Feeborn was all long and lean and graceful with 'fine bones' according to Auntie Paula.

Well, how come Grandpa Freeborn gets into Rosalee's egg, eh, when I get, God knows who – probably some malicious deformed-nos-triled throwback who's been hanging round for the past couple of thousand years *just waiting* to launch his obscene orifices on some poor unsuspecting Freeborn, me! How come I get *him* in *my* egg, that's what I'd like to know? And thinking about all this I got a great heavy feeling in my chest that sat there for a bit and then travelled down to my stomach. A sort of ache. It just wasn't right. The sheer *accidentalness* of it seemed so unfair.

So even though it was about four hundred degrees in the shade I pulled my curtains, put on my bedside light and got stuck into the last eighteen pages of W. H. Only eighteen pages left! Where will I go to seek refuge from these sudden cruel revelations? I'll have to find another escape route – maybe *Jane Eyre* or *Gone with the Wind*, or something.

Alexa, do you think I'm vain and selfish? Or is this a stage that most teenagers go through, a sort of anxiety phase? Looking forward to hearing your views on this important matter.

Love

Gilly

PS   What is rhinoplasty? It sounds like something to do with modelling rhinoceroses, but I think it's to do with reshaping noses, isn't it?

23 Tudor Avenue
Benbridge
Trowton TR0 9AF

Ms Alexa Deerheart   7 July
THE BIZZ

Dear Alexa

Well, I'm glad you didn't give me the standard 'everyone is different' answer, though you're probably right when you say that when I feel happier about myself generally I won't even think about my ginormous camel flares. They're not going to go away, are they?

I fainted on Thursday. My heart stopped. It pounded in my chest at about a zillion beats a second and then just *stopped*. Emily said I turned neon puce and then a pale shade of white and then passed out on the floor in the middle of assembly.

I blamed the heat; the stifling atmosphere of closed windows in 100° temperature, and the drone of Pennings' speech about 'young people entering a new decade' and how we had 'such a responsibility' (I was thinking *exactly*! You hypocrite, all false words, but when it comes to the crunch . . . just wait until you see the Trowton *Echo*). That was what I was thinking when Pennings suddenly said, 'And I am inviting some of our forward-looking young people up here to give us a few thoughts on the future. . . .'

I wasn't prepared. There HE was, suddenly. On the stage, wearing a blue cotton jacket. His tie was undone, his shirt open at the neck. He began reciting a *poem* – it was something about:

What are days for/Days are where we live

He was saying all these profound and poetic things, and I felt like shouting, 'I'm a poet too.' I was so worked up, but instead I crashed to the ground, overcome. This is getting *really* dangerous, Alexa. Where will it all end? But, can you imagine, he's not only beautiful and clever and funny, but he likes *poetry*, too! Our minds are in harmony!

Love

Gilly Freeborn

23 *Tudor Avenue*
Benbridge
Trowton TR0 9AF

Ms Alexa Deerheart   10 July
THE BIZZ

Dear Alexa

I . . . listened to the soft wind breathing through the
grass, and wondered how any one could ever imagine
unquiet slumbers for the sleepers in that quiet earth.

Good, eh? That's not me, though. It's Emily,
finishing off *Wuthering Heights*. I feel sort of
stranded now. Deserted. I knew I would. The
thing I've discovered is that however bad you
feel, if you've got a book you can sort of disappear into it, and the whole world can be
hammering on the outside saying stuff like,
'You're not eating the right things/you'll never
get anywhere if you don't *work*/you've got
stubby legs and pimples/nobody likes you/you
look too young/no, you can't have any new
clothes until you've put in some solid maths
revision', they can call you 'snot nose' and
'creepy spy' and 'amoeba brain' and 'angst-
ridden prepubescent' and all the time you can
be walking on a 'fresh watery afternoon, when
turf and paths were rustling with moist with-
ered leaves' or being told 'I'd as soon forget

158

you, as my existence!' in passionate tones, and they just can't get in. They're stuck on the outside like people on the television with the sound turned down.

So anyway, I've started my essay. It's going to be the best thing I've ever done. And I'm going to start it off with a poem to Emily. Good idea? Sometimes I think she's looking down on us, amazed to see all these people in funny clothes reading her book. Maybe she is. I'd really like her to know that I think she's pretty good. That she's kept me going through some pretty sticky moments. I'm going to write an even better essay than the Brain of Britain. And somehow I know that I can, funnily enough.

Love

Gilly

23 *Tudor Avenue*
Benbridge
Trowton TR0 9AF

Ms Alexa Deerheart   13 July
THE BIZZ

Dear Alexa

I've got something! Something of HIS. Something that has been upon his body. Something that has absorbed his human perfume.

I was in the changing room after gym, where Mrs Brake had, for some reason known only to God and the Physical Education Board for 11–15-year-olds, been making us climb up the wall and down again. Then, when we were nice and sweaty, we had to join hands with our partners and stick our legs in the air like some sort of hydrophobic synchronized swimming team. I suppose she thought it was 'fun' because we were doing it to music – some ancient pop ballad from 1978 or something. We looked downright *daft*, standing there in our shorts and T-shirts, wobbling about on one leg.

Anyway, I leapt in the shower afterwards, keeping my arms crossed over my chest like an angel in the Christmas play. I hate seeing all those bosoms; even poor Phyllis's undersized brain is orchestrating her glands through the concerto of puberty. *She's* got bumps; small but evident. As for Judy, well, hers are *flagrant*, and she struts around in her perfect naked body with perfect confidence, her towel draped randomly about her frame, her silky wet hair combed back to show off her perfect shell-like ears studded with tiny gold stars that were a love gift from HIM, as we've heard a thousand times and more. She's already left us, really. She seems out of place among our gaggle of gangly teenagers. She could step out tomorrow, gracefully and surely, into the world of the adult. She could sit sipping champagne by some yup's swimming pool and no one would think, 'There's an angst-ridden adolescent' – not one person; it wouldn't even cross their minds.

I didn't feel like talking to anyone. Gym was our last lesson. I watched Annie link arms with Brainbox, not without a pang of jealousy (so, OK, I've admitted it). Sarryan and Emily are all right, but it's not the same as having your very own personal best friend who you can tell practically anything to (well, almost) and who will take your side against the world, even when you're in the wrong. It's just not the same. Sarry and Em had gone, anyway, drifted off in their own perfect best-friendship – they don't always remember to remember me.

So I sat there for a while, my hair dripping raindrops on to my shoulders and down the back of my blazer. I put my Walkman on and listened to *Who Will Love This Lonely Heart* by the French Sisters, who've got these fantastic deep soulful voices that shoot through your bones and land in your toes with a tingling sensation. I was thinking about HIM, about Judy, about Annie and Sarryan and Emily, about Mum and Dad, about Rosalee's ankles, about my giant nostrils, about my essay on *Wuthering Heights*, and about Pennings letting us down about LSHYWAC. I was thinking about all these things and the French Sisters were echoing my thoughts with:

> *Oh Sister, who will love this lonely heart;*
> *Who will bother even try-i-ing,*
> *When it's so torn and bitter, full of hurt,*
> *Been used and now it's sigh-i-ing.*
> *Whaaa—wha—whaaaaaaaaaa!*

I stayed until the last 'Whaaaa' then slung my bag over my shoulder, made sure everyone had gone and made my way out.

Something, heaven knows what, made me push back the open door that separates the boys' changing room from ours. And there, behind the door, on the polished blue mosaic tiles alone and solitary stood – a black Puma sportsbag! I didn't have to look at the name tag. I knew that bag! I knew its shiny contours.

I must have stood looking at it for a full two minutes, almost in awe. It seemed to *glow* as if it contained some mysterious, magical power,

162

some promise, like Ali Baba's lamp, instead of just a blue and green football shirt and shorts. I knew that somehow Plan B had been presented to me by Fate. But what to do? Should I look for him now and receive his grateful thanks. No. *She* would be with him and my gesture would be wasted, nullified by a withering look. I picked it up, stuffed it under my blazer and walked out of the door. I looked right, then left then strode down the corridor with the sportsbag clasped fast to my chest while the French Sisters sang 'Grab it while you've got the chance/Baby it never come round twice/Do do, step-it-up, step-it-up/Baby you've got to move it now!'

We had beefburgers and chips for tea. Fantastic. I think I'm a real living paradox – I mean, it's a dilemma. There can't be many strict vegetarians whose favourite food is beefburgers and chips, can there? Mum looked thrilled when I asked for more. Really, it's pathetic. Then it suddenly struck me! She thinks I'm getting anorexia. And then I felt bad. Anorexia's really serious. I read about it in *The Bizz*. When you look in the mirror you see yourself as about ten times fatter than you really are. A girl in 10b had it and had to go to hospital. She was force-fed through a tube with carrots and shepherd's pie. And then I began to wonder if I *did* have it. So I looked in the mirror that night, thinking that maybe I really did have long graceful legs and tiny ankles and Grandpa Freeborn's bones, and that I was just *seeing* this shortish, moon-faced person with puppy fat around the waist. But then I felt hungry and went downstairs and ate a whole angel cake and a dollop of cream. So I don't think I have got it, do you, Alexa?

The Adidas bag was under my bed. I could feel its presence as I walked into my room. It was almost *alive*. I put out the big light, angled my Anglepoise, unzipped the bag and examined the contents one by one. The football shirt, the black shorts, a green towel, a wrist band, the *snow-white socks*, a half-finished packet of fruit pastilles, a pen, a clean pair of boxer shorts! I think I had been hoping for a notebook, something that harboured his secret thoughts, something that said 'I've seen this girl in 9a' or 'Judy's beginning to get on my nerves' or 'I was in the hairdresser's when this amazing girl just told them all where to get off'. But of course this was just one of my pitiful fantasies, my silly, self-deceiving daydreams that have no foundation in the sharp, cruel realness of the world.

Anyway, Alexa, I held his things close to me, I wrapped my arms around them, breathed deep the scent of his bodily juices. If only I could *have* something, I thought. Some small thing of HIS to keep and cherish, to help me feel his presence. Then it came to me. A

SOCK! A single pure white cotton sock that had lived upon his precious foot. He wouldn't miss it. After all, people are always losing socks, aren't they? The world is full of solitary socks, whose partners have upped and left them lying forgotten and useless at the bottom of linen baskets and launderette bags. So, I folded my prize, emptied my glass bead collection from the antique silver trinket box that Grandma Freeborn gave me, and put it inside. It now lies in a special place at the bottom of my wardrobe. A sock in a box.

I repacked the bag this morning. Plan B needs much deep and careful thought. My brain is certainly working flat out at the moment. Click, click, clicking over in ponderance of many momentous questions of grave consequence.

Love

Gilly

23 Tudor Avenue
Benbridge
Trowton TR0 9AF

Ms Alexa Deerheart   15 July
THE BIZZ

Dear Alexa

> Emily's footsteps
> Were long and light.
> Fairy footsteps
> Hardly there.
> Over moors she went
> Making paths
> For us to follow.

Then I go on to talk about how that lonely home and *secret love* (the Gillian Freeborn Theory) must have been the inspiration for *Wuthering Heights*. And then there was her unique character which was 'stronger than a man's and simpler than a child's' to quote her sister Charlotte, and stuff like that. And once I had started writing I couldn't stop. I even took my books to bed with me and wrote on my lap. I reread my favourite bits, like when Heathcliff comes back transformed with his half-civilized ferocity lurking in eyes full of black fire!

Then about half-past one Rosalee went to the loo and of course she couldn't help sticking her head round the door, squinty-eyed and suspicious, in the hope of catching me in the middle of some furtive undercover activity that she could report to Mum. 'God, you're not doing *homework*, are you?' she hissed. 'Wonders will never cease. Isn't your brain hurting under the strain? I think I can see your head caving in!'

But I just stuck my tongue out. Really, you wouldn't think she'd be able to keep it up, night and day, day and night, continual persecution and harassment. You'd think she'd get tired of the sound of her own drone.

Anyway, Alexa, I've written *thirteen and a half* pages! I know I shouldn't say it but it isn't bad, really. I keep wondering how many pages Brainbox has written, and whether she's been having the same ideas as me.

It's lying in a folder at the bottom of my wardrobe. A blue folder that I bought specially. It's lying there next to THE BOX. Whenever I'm feeling fed up, or lump-like, or pathetic or insignificant or whatever, I just think of them, there together, like two talismen of achievement.

The essays have to be in by Friday. Keep your fingers crossed.

Love

Gilly

PS   I saw Tracey striding towards the library carrying a HUGE green folder. I bet it's her essay. I don't care how big her folder is, though, it's what's inside that counts.

23 Tudor Avenue
Benbridge
Trowton TR0 9AF

Ms Alexa Deerheart   20 July
THE BIZZ

Dear Alexa

Plan B has happened. It has taken place. It went like this: Monday. For the first time in the history of the world I felt pleased that we were having home ec. We had the choice of making spaghetti savoury bake or cheese and potato pie, so nobody thought it particularly unusual when I arrived lugging Dad's big holdall over my shoulder and nearly breaking my bones under the strain. 'God, whatonearth you got in there?' said Sarry as she watched me unload my precious baggage in the classroom.

'Potatoes, of course!' I said with perfect equanimity. 'For the pie.'

Sarry snorted. 'Cor, *some* pie! I've only got three. Miss said that would be enough.'

'Well,' I said mysteriously, 'you can never be sure with potatoes. Especially, King Edwards.'

I left the holdall in class, the black Adidas bag inside buried by two pounds of King Edward Specials, a bag inside a bag, and rushed to assembly. I took my place next to Annie in the choir. Mrs Biles struck up the piano and we launched into 'How my glorious burden makes light my poor and humble heart'. Annie and I sang our harmonies really strongly. I sounded lovely. At least Brainbox can't sing, I was thinking to myself, at least that's one thing she can't do.

My stomach was jumping about so much it was almost taking on a life of its own. My chest pounded and my head reeled at the thought of the task ahead, my plan. First thing after assembly I double-checked the big timetable outside Pennings' office. 11a's last lesson of the day was biology, then there was football practice for the team. There was *half an hour* between class finishing and the practice. Half an hour in which I could be pretty sure of finding him alone, if I moved fast enough.

The whole day passed in a haze. I couldn't concentrate on my cheese and potato pie. Mrs Gupta said that cookery was not one of my natural talents, which I could have told her anyway. Phyllis was making the spaghetti savoury bake, which as far as I could see involved boiling a pan of spaghetti then pouring a heated-up tin of tomatoes over it and slapping on some cheese. My pie didn't even look like food. It looked like a sort of demoralized Frisbee with anaemia. I could see Sarryan looking at me strangely, trying to figure out how a whole bag of King Edwards could reduce to such a sad, flat thing.

The afternoon seemed to last forever, eternity. Finally, after an hour of sweltering in history drawing a chart of the kings and queens of England, the bell went. I rushed to the classroom, retrieved my holdall and fled to the lab with my heart in my mouth. It was now or never.

He was sitting there reading, all alone. The back of his head is one of the most beautiful things I've ever seen – dark with luscious black curls twisting and intertwining with each other like silken coils. I stood in the doorway mesmerized, palpitating, my heart like a hydraulic pressure pump, a road drill, a high-speed xpress train. I walked towards him, slowly, the silence ringing like church bells in my ears. He didn't hear. As if guided by some ethereal force, my hand reached out and touched his shoulder.

'Oh,' he said, turning round, 'it's the rebel hairdresser.'

'Eeeink,' I squeaked, overcome.

'Well,' he said. 'What can I do for you?'

'I found this,' I replied in squeaky tones. 'I found it in the street at lunchtime. It's got your name on it.'

'Oh, great!' he said. 'Fantastic. I thought I'd left it in the gym and it'd been stolen. Hey, thanks! But how come it was in the street? That's really weird.'

'Dunno,' I said. 'Perhaps someone *did* steal it, someone who didn't like sport and changed their mind when they saw the football things.'

'Yeah,' he said giving me a funny look. 'Very strange. I'd better check that there's nothing missing.'

'Well, curiouser and curiouser,' he said. 'Everything's here except ... a sock!' (Oh, God! I was thinking. Scuppered!) 'I know!' he went on. 'The ruthless sock thief of Trowton must be on the loose again. He's a real desperado. He'll stop at nothing to get his mitts on a nice fresh piece of hosiery.'

He was smiling.

I was smiling.

I was melting.

It was a moment in time to record in my brain and replay late at night to fuel my dreams. Then all of a sudden Judy Fry was in the doorway, looking at us, furious.

'Hey, Judy,' he said. 'Guess what? My bag has been found.'

If looks could kill. If her eyes could have leapt out their sockets and burned me through, they would have. But I didn't care. I had had my moment. Plan B had worked. Something I had planned had actually worked.

All things must change, Alexa. He can't love Judy for ever, can he?

Love

Gilly

PS   I'm handing my essay in tomorrow. Twenty pages! I've done a crayon drawing of Haworth Parsonage and a watercolour portrait of Emily copied from a library book. I've tried really hard.

23 *Tudor Avenue*
Benbridge
Trowton TR0 9AF

Ms Alexa Deerheart   24 July
THE BIZZ

Dear Alexa

Saturday afternoon. Mum was out at Doreen's. Rosalee was working at ZAP. Dad was in his herb garden harvesting his garlic and spraying everything with Ultra-Safe Ozone-Friendly Bug Killer, though how anything that kills caterpillars, the embryo butterflies, the future kings of the garden, can be friendly, I don't know. I took Sarryan's dad's cassette out of my bag, put it in Dad's tape deck and cranked the volume up to number seven.

> *Millions of people swarming*
> *Like flies round Waterloo underground*

went blasting through the wide-open window. I watched Dad from a safe place behind the curtain. All of a sudden he stopped spraying, stood stock-still and stared out across the flat, dry gardens of Benbridge, a bulb of garlic in his hand. It was working!

I threw myself on the sofa and affected an attitude of serious, concentrated grooving.

Within seconds he was at the window, leaning through.

Terry and Julie
Da-da-da-da-da-da

'Good heavens!' said Dad. 'Where on earth did you get that?'

'Sarryan lent it to me,' I said. 'It's the latest thing. Sixties music is making a comeback. They're playing it in all the clubs.'

'Well, I never,' said Dad. 'This takes me back a few years.'

'Does it remind you of anything, anyone?' I said in subtle tones, trying not to be too obvious.

'My goodness, it does,' said Dad. Then an expression of distant, long-forgotten bliss came over his face. 'Beryl Potts! Beryl Potts in the back of my dad's Ford Cortina – my goodness, were *they* cars.'

Beryl Potts! Beryl *Potts*! I cast back into the shadowy outreaches of his romantic past, and came up with some sweaty back seat of the car experience with someone called *Potts*. I'd gone too far. 'Dad,' I said with a look of innocent inquisitiveness, 'when did you meet Mum?'

'Oh, about 1972,' he said gruffly, the spell broken. He turned back to his indiscriminate murdering of garden life, singing, '*Whenever I gaze on Waterloo sunset, I am in paradise.*'

I'll just have to do more research. Be more

devious. Still, at least the power of music has proved itself. I'll get a tape of the Greatest Hits of 1972. That should get him going.

I just *cannot* believe it! I'm doomed, marked out by some venomous messenger of Fate whose sole mission in the otherworld is to manipulate Chance to throw the most humiliating and cringe-making experiences my way.

After school on Monday I was going to town to meet Mum so she could buy me a new swimming costume and a pair of shorts for our holiday (of course, there was a sale in Marks and Spencer). I was just getting on the 32b, when Phyllis came lumbering up, all sweaty and out of breath, spluttering out something about having to go to the foot clinic and could she sit next to me.

And there I was, sitting on the long seat with Phyllis slobbering all over me and squashing me into the corner when who should get on at the next stop? Who should get on and sit right opposite us? Who should be the one person in the world to experience the misguided affection of a slobbering ignoramic jellyfish being lavished upon one who has done nothing *really* bad in life and who when alone presents a pretty well normal and dignified impression to the world. Yes, of course. HE.

I tried to hide by squashing myself even further into the corner, keeping my head down

174

and letting my fringe fall over my face (a much used ploy). And it would have *worked* if the bus hadn't given a horrible juddery jolt which caused Phyllis's school bag to fall open on her lap. Then all of a sudden there was this ghastly nostril-rotting *smell*. It was like rancid tuna fish and drains and lavatories all mixed together. People were coughing and spluttering and I was nearly gagging with the stench when I noticed this STUFF wriggling across Phyllis's lap and oozing on to the floor. A sort of seething waterfall of wriggling worms slolloping and slurping down her skirt and sliding across the floor to attack other passengers. It was as if she were emitting some sort of soft stringy fetid ectoplasm with tentacles. The whole mess was embroiled in a sort of red *mould* and all the time Phyllis was just sitting there, staring at HIM with her usual inane yellow tooth grin as if nothing was happening. Then I realized. Oh, God! The spaghetti savoury bake! The spaghetti savoury bake had been festering in Phyllis's bag for *four* days and had chosen *this* precise moment to break free of its Tupperware box and launch itself on the world. And the conductor stopped the bus and started shouting and Phyllis started crying and HE was gagging and choking and all the while looking at me with an expression of utter disgust and incredulity on his face. And I felt like crying out, 'She's nothing to do with me!' which was pretty pointless as she was hanging on to me in a vice-like grip and going 'Gilly, Gilly!' in whinging tones.

Well, to avoid dwelling on this tragic story, I'll just tell you that I had to get off the bus with her, two stops early, and calm her down. I helped her clean up as best I could and walked her back home.

Mum was *furious,* not surprisingly as she'd spent an hour waiting for me outside Marks and Spencer with a 'just the thing' swimming costume in mind.

Alexa, only a week to go. Only a week for me to redeem myself; to erase his memory of me as bosom friend to a dribbling, sausage-oozing, putrid-spaghetti ejecting nerdette. I hope you don't think I'm mean to Phyllis. I *do* feel sorry for her, but that doesn't mean I want her following me through my life ejecting unidentified matter at crucial moments.

I've just *got* to win the essay competition now! That's the one thing that may restore my dignity and give him a glimpse of a higher, sensitive mind.

Love

Gilly

23 *Tudor Avenue*
Benbridge
Trowton TR0 9AF

Ms Alexa Deerheart   26 July
THE BIZZ

Dear Alexa

Sometimes I feel like nothing. A great big fat ugly nothing mound of flesh that might just as well go and curl up and expire somewhere in some out-of-the-way place where no one could find me. Who would care, anyway? I'm never going to be beautiful. Or clever. Or interesting. Or artistic. Or creative. Never. Mum is right. I'll never be anything but a big lazy lump. There's absolutely no point to me being on the earth and using up its precious resources when there are more deserving cases, like slugs or lugworms.

This is how I was feeling after Rosalee came bounding home screaming that she'd won a competition in ZAP for writing the best advertising slogan for the local paper. I know I should have been pleased, but why does she have to have everything? Why does she have to be pretty and thin and graceful *and* then go and win a competition for writing? She's never been even *remotely* interested in writing before.

But you see, Alexa, the essay results are on

177

Friday, our last day. I've just got to win, because if I don't it means all the above is true and I may as well go and lie down in the middle of the M4 motorway and get run over by a ten-ton articulated lorry.

Love

Gilly

23 Tudor Avenue
Benbridge
Trowton TR0 9AF

Ms Alexa Deerheart   28 July
THE BIZZ

Dear Alexa

It's Friday evening. School is over. Finished
for six weeks. I expect you're on tenterhooks,
wanting to know what happened with the prize.
Well, I'm exhausted, worn out. It went like
this:

We were supposed to be having normal
lessons in the morning, but because it was the
last day we didn't do any real work. I suppose
all the teachers were just as jittery as we were,
waiting to escape the confines of Langley Street
High and catch their planes to Torremolinos
or wherever it is they go. It was hot, hot, hot
again and I couldn't think of anything but the
prizegiving. I kept seeing my folder, blue and
vulnerable, lying there waiting for its final
judgement. So the morning was *torture*. I tried
hard to be relaxed but at break Sarryan said,
'What's up, Gilly? You seem a bit wound up.'

'Too hot,' I said. 'I don't feel well,' which
was true. I was sweating and twitching; one
minute getting a great surge of excitement at
the thought of walking on stage to collect my

prize, and the next being thrust down thinking, It'll *never* happen. Brainbox'll win – she always does.

And all through English I watched Mrs Goldstein closely, to see if I could get a hint, a sign of what was coming. To see if I could read something into a look, a gesture. But she wasn't giving anything away, nothing. She just said, 'Well, girls, well done with all your essays. Only another hour to go and you'll be out of your misery.'

I don't remember much about the first part. I just remember the buzz of about three hundred kids stuck inside on a hot afternoon while outside six whole weeks of freedom waited.

I remember Parrot Beak Parkins saying something about the best maths class he'd had for years and as long as they kept up the good work it could be a record year for GCSEs. Big deal, I remember thinking. Who cares. Fractions, equations, logarithms – ugly black things, soul-killers, all of them. And suddenly we were there. Judgement time. My heart beat was accelerating, my hands were twisting round each other in a sweaty mess. Let it be me. Let it be me, I was thinking. Only, this is something I really want. And old hypocrite Pennings was going on about Mrs Goldstein's English prize and how this annual event had turned up some very excellent work in the past and how it really did help us to prepare for the hard GCSE work ahead. And on and on about *Wuthering Heights* and how it was one of the best novels in the English language, as if we didn't know that already. And of course he was saying how difficult the decision had been because the standard was so very high, but finally, after a great deal of discussion and careful thought, the prize goes to . . .

'Tracey Mann for "*Wuthering Heights, dissected*" which is a highly accomplished academic work, especially impressive as the author is only fourteen years old. Well done, Tracey!'

I know you have to face disappointments in the world, but sometimes it's too hard. I thought my heart would break – burst through my chest and drop on the floor. Nothing seemed worth anything. I felt as if I might as well just give up trying to do anything ever again, if I couldn't even tell what was good and what was rubbish. I thought about Emily's poem, and how I had really *meant* it, and if something you *really mean* doesn't mean anything to anyone else, what's it worth? Oh, and all this was going round in my brain and I was sinking, falling back two, three, five, ten years until I was four years old again and thinking, 'It's not fair! It's not fair! Not fair! My life is ruined, finished.' And getting redder and hotter as I felt the stupid baby tears coming, welling up. Pennings was still droning on and on, but I wasn't listening. I just had this loud buzzing in my ears that was blocking out the world and leaving me floating around in the middle of nowhere. Then the words 'special prize' broke through my silent torture. Special prize.

'This year,' he was saying, 'we have taken the unusual step of awarding a "special prize" for what we have decided to call an "exceptional piece of writing". Although this essay doesn't have the depth of research or the breadth of academic argument of the winning entry, it *does* have an energy and *heart* which really touches the reader and somehow gets across a real enthusiasm both for the book and the author. And that prize goes to . . . Gillian Freeborn for *"Emily's Footsteps"*.' Applause! Applause for Gillian Freeborn, short, unformed, unbeautiful, angst-ridden Gillian Freeborn. Me. My name.

Altered states. One minute I'm floundering about in the pit of failure; the next I'm walking up the platform steps to collect a prize. Mrs Goldstein's smile is touching both ears and even Mr Parkins has forgotten his logarithms and is clapping away like mad.

Back at my seat, I looked at my prize. It was a hardback copy of *Pride and Prejudice* by Jane Austen with a flowery label inside that said 'Awarded to Gillian Freeborn, 10a, the Special Prize for her outstanding essay *"Emily's Footsteps"*.' I was thinking about telling Mum and Dad, I was thinking about saying, 'I got the *Special Prize*' when something made me turn round. Annie was looking at me. Actually looking me straight in the eye for the first time in months. And I don't know why, but I smiled, I smiled a sort of lop-sided grin into the air and hoped that she'd catch it and throw it back. *And she did.* It was just like something familiar and comfortable coming back, like the time I found my old blue teddy squashed down the back of the sofa.

And walking out, Sarry and Em came up and said, 'Well done, Gilly. That's one in the eye for Brainy Pants. They obviously *liked* yours best. It's about time she fell off her high horse.' And we said goodbye and promised to ring each other in the holidays and Phyllis came over and dribbled all over me, and I felt quite fond of her, really.

Then Mrs Goldstein called me. 'Well, Gilly,' she said. 'I can't say that I wasn't surprised. That was a lovely piece of work.'

'Do you really think so?' I said, wallowing. I mean, I haven't had many chances to bask in glory in my life. Or any, come to that.

'Yes, I do,' she went on. 'I didn't know you had it in you. We'll be expecting a lot from you next term.'

And I thought, How can you know what's in me? Or what's in anyone, for that matter? Deep down there could be anything – for all we know even Phyllis could have a spark of something hidden in that lanky, gangling frame. It'd have to be pretty deep, I admit. But for all we know she could have a great talent for finger painting or car mechanics or bird charming – *anything* could be buried down there.

Then in a moment of rashness, I said, 'I've written some poems too. Would you like to see them?'

And she could hardly say no because I took my blue book out of my bag, shoved it in her hand and ran down the corridor at a hundred miles an hour before I could change my mind. I was in some strange place between the earth and the sky, walking on air, I suppose.

I went back to the classroom to pack up my stuff. Everyone had gone, or so I thought. I was folding up my painting of 'Ellen Pugh with Carnations' to take home when I sensed there was someone in the room.

'Hello,' said Annie.

'Hello,' I said, looking down.

'Can I see your prize?' she asked.

'If you like,' I said casually. And I gave her my *Pride and Prejudice* with the label that said 'For her outstanding essay . . .' inside.

And she stood there, red in the face, just looking at it, not saying anything. I suppose neither of us wanted to be the first.

'Sorry!' she blurted out suddenly, just like that. And I said, 'I'm sorry too,' and burst into tears. Then Annie burst into tears as well. 'I'm sorry I was so *stupid*,' she said. 'No, I was stupid,' I said. 'We're best friends,' said Annie. 'Nothing should break us up. I was just stupid, stupid and jealous.'

And then I just grabbed her and gave her a great big hug! 'Let's not ever split up again, ever, ever,' I said.

'Not *ever*,' said Annie.

'I love you best,' I said.

'I love you,' said Annie.

And that was that. I suppose you think this is pretty soppy stuff, Alexa. I hope you don't show my letters to anyone. It may seem soppy, but it's *very private* and important. And I'm only telling you because I want to tell someone how fantastic it is to have your very best friend back.

Mum and Dad were thrilled about the prize. Mum was smiling like mad, but desperately trying not to go over the top. She's not keen on things 'going to people's heads'. Dad just said, 'Well done, Gillykins. You know where you get your brains from.' And Mum said, 'A lot of good they'll do her if she turns out like you.' But she wasn't *really* serious. She was sort of smiling. It was great. My 'Greatest Hits of the Seventies' must be having an effect.

So we're off tomorrow. Off to the hotel with the swimming pool and the giant water chute. Half of me is looking forward to this holiday.

The other half is soul-sick at the thought of a whole three weeks without the chance of a glimpse, the chance of a chance meeting. The chance of love's young dream leaping out of bushes and striking HIM smack between the eyes. But I'm taking 'the box'. I've already put it in my case wrapped up in a towel. If I hold it and meditate, I may be able to bring him to my mind's sight – oh glorious one!

I'll send you a postcard.

Love

Gillian Freeborn (prizewinner!)

Ms Alexa Deerheart   5 August
THE BIZZ

Dear Alexa

I thought I might as well write to you properly.
After all, I am lying here entombed in Cala-
mine lotion and a wet beach towel while Mum
and Dad are lying on the golden sands of Flaya
Paradisimo turning a crispy golden brown and
Rosalee is probably strutting the beach in her
new blue and black zigzag swimming costume
with the hole in the front drawing drooling
glances from manhood all and sundry.

And I've been sleeping and waking, waking
and sleeping in a strange dream-ridden feverish
way. All my life seems to be flicking back and
forwards and the real bits keep getting mixed
up with the dream bits and sometimes I wake
up not knowing who or where I am. And the
bits about HIM are the best, the bits where
I'm floating in some trailing gauzy stuff, white
and shining, and he comes floating in from the
other direction and we collide and start to
dance like they do in those old black and white
films. And in another one I was on the beach

and he was rubbing suntan lotion all over me, very slowly, down my arms and legs and on my back. And I woke up feeling *ever so funny*. I could still *feel* him doing it – the sensation. And then I began thinking, I don't know anything. I don't know, for instance, what *men* feel like, what sort of feelings they get. I'd really like to know.

I saw a bit of this film once. I was supposed to be watching 'The Sound of Music' but I thought, What a load of twaddle, and turned over. At first I thought I'd tuned into some video nasty, an illegal horror cable programme that had somehow got into our telly by mistake. This man was lying on a bed making funny grunting noises, like a pig with constipation. And although you couldn't see a woman, you knew there was one there because these high-pitched squeaky noises that sounded like a rat gasping were coming from underneath him. And the man was doing *press-ups* on top of her – it looked as if he were trying to gyrate her to a pulp. And then he started doing these press-ups really fast and huffing and puffing and going 'Eyore! Eyore!' like a donkey. And when the woman started going, 'Yes, yes, darling! Oh! Oh! Ooooo!' it suddenly clicked. They were *doing it*. And I thought, I never imagined it like *that*. It looked so bloody ridiculous. No wonder they call men animals, although animals probably have more sense and do it quickly and quietly to get it over with.

Then Mum came in, worse luck, and went purple and said, 'Well, "The Sound of Music" has certainly changed since I was a girl,' and snapped off the button and told me to get upstairs and what on earth was the BBC coming to because it was only a quarter to ten and it just wasn't on.

I expect you know all this stuff, Alexa. But what I'd really like to know is, what was the man *feeling*? Why was he making those funny noises? Now I'm getting to understand it a bit, I imagine the woman was having some sort of intensified *spasms*. But what was the man having? And why was he doing press-ups? Why not just lie still and let nature take its course? Anyway, I looked up 'ejaculation' in the dictionary, thinking this might explain the sensation. But it just said: *'an unmeditated emotional prayer; to emit semen'*. I mean, talk about confusing. Why should you pray while you're doing it, eh? And what happens if you're an atheist? What do you do then? It sounds daft to me.

Mum says it'll take about three days for this burning, itching skin to mend. It's got to peel off, ugh! I'm feeling ever so strange, Alexa. I feel like I don't know anything.

Yours in delirium

Gilly

Ms Alexa Deerheart   16 August
THE BIZZ

Dear Alexa

Do you know how it feels to lose about three metres of your outer body? I'll tell you, bloody awful. It all fell off in ribbons leaving me red and raw and blistered. I looked like the Creature Whose Skin Fell Off. It's gone down a bit now and I'm a sort of reddy brown colour, the first time in my life I've been anything but Cornish pasty white. And even though I wasn't completely better, Rosalee made me go to a disco, just so she could have a fat red blob standing next to her to make her own thin brown body look even more marvellous in comparison. And, of course, it worked. Two boys would approach us. One would ask Rosalee to dance, the other would look at me in disgust as if I was a dead cat or something. And nine times out of ten, they weren't even good-looking. And sometimes they were downright ugly and *small*. And I'd think, Who do you think you are, rotten slimy creeps, I wouldn't want to dance with you anyway, and there are a lot more appealing things in life than being mauled by your sweaty mitts.

But I really did mind, Alexa. It's pathetic, isn't it? And I kept going to the loo and wandering round but I felt so *stupid*. And in the end I went outside, walked up a hill and sat on the grass. There was just me, then. I sat there looking at the stars, meditating on *Wuthering Heights* and thinking if you wrote a book like that you wouldn't care about anything. You wouldn't care about some spotty, slimy creeps with sweaty armpits asking you to dance. You'd tell them all to get lost. I stayed there for an hour and a half. I didn't care. Rosalee didn't even notice that I'd gone. Luckily I had my pencil in my bag to record the poignant moment:

> *Oh, fat lumpish, sun-scorched one*
> *Cruelly used, then scorned*
> *By youth's shallow sight.*
> *Take no heed! Turn thy face*
> *For deeper things lurk*
> *Within your beating breast.*

Just a quick note. I don't *think* I'm imagining it. I was in the bath when I thought I could see these swelling mounds rising above the foam. I didn't want to get too excited. I didn't want to shout, 'Oh, *thank you*, God!' before I was sure. You know I've been disappointed before. So I moved position and thrust my chest through the foam again. But they seemed to disappear. Then I relaxed, changed position again, shut my eyes and opened them again quickly, hoping to catch them unawares. And there was definitely *something there*. Then I examined myself in the mirror, sideways, and I didn't go *straight* down, there was a slight sloping, ever so slight, but there. I can *feel* them. They feel sort of muscly. And I reckoned everything must have got going when I was in bed, sweltering and sweating and peeling. It must have helped to accelerate the process. It was probably the sun-cream dream that gave them their final boost.

I'll write as soon as I get home and let you know the latest.

Fingers crossed

Love

Gilly

PS   A boy looked at me yesterday. Stared. I thought he must have been looking at Rosalee, but when I turned round she wasn't there. She was admiring herself in a shop window. He wasn't bad-looking, either.

23 Tudor Avenue
Benbridge
Trowton TR0 9AF

Ms Alexa Deerheart   23 August
THE BIZZ

Dear Alexa

They've come! They've come! I've got them!
They're here! My bumps. Nothing's going to
stop them now. It's not a mistake or wishful
thinking. They're there in pink and white. I
tried on Rosalee's pink Spandex when she was
out and I didn't look ridiculous at all. They
showed. They stuck out. Mum says I don't
need a bra yet, but I'm going to get one anyway.
I mean, you don't know how big they're going
to get. Alexa, I've got a tan, *and* bumps!

We got home really late on Sunday night.
Both Rosalee and I were immediately cast
down into deepest gloom. Rosalee because
she'd left Pepé, her swarthy dark conquest,
behind in Alcudia and felt like having a brow-
wiping-locking-herself-in-her-room experience
while composing the story she would be telling
to everybody at ZAP about her tragic forced
separation to make them raving mad with jealousy. (She didn't even ring poor Cliff, who
seems to have been exiled to oblivion in the
wake of new passions.) Me, because Benbridge

193

seemed like the wasteland of the soul after the wonders of Spain, especially as it was raining and they've started building that health club in the one and only field we've got left.

But there were two excitements. The first is that there was a letter from Sarryan *with a newspaper clipping* inside. They printed our letter! They printed our letter in the Trowton *Evening Echo*. They took their time, but there it was, in black and white, our names. And somehow the *best* thing was seeing Phyllis's name in print. Phyllis Bean. Phyllis Bean has been famous, if only for a day. For some reason this was almost better than anything. I can't wait to hear what old hypocrite worm Pennings has to say about it. Dad said that we were dead right and he'd stick by me every inch of the way. And Mum said, 'Gilly, I never knew you had it in you,' which just goes to show you, Alexa, just how little people know about your insides.

The second amazing thing was we also had a letter from Auntie Paula. She's getting married! And not to the dreaded Tom, either. It's someone called Fred who no one's ever heard of. And Dad was laughing and Mum seemed really pleased and kept saying, 'Well I never,' and 'It's about time,' and 'I bet she's pregnant,' and Dad said, 'So what?' And Alexa, I thought, So what? too. I'll have a cousin.

The wedding is in three weeks' time. It's in a register office in the country, near Grandma

Freeborn. I'm going to get a new dress. Mum's ever so pleased, although I don't know why it's such a big deal.

I really wanted to see Annie, but she was in France on holiday. So I rang Sarryan instead. We're going to meet in the Fresh Bake on Saturday. Only two weeks of freedom left!

Love

an almost fully formed

Gilly

23 Tudor Avenue
Benbridge
Trowton TR0 9AF

Ms Alexa Deerheart   27 August
THE BIZZ

Dear Alexa

Ten days to go. Ten days until I know for definite that I'll be seeing him again. Be within touching distance. It's a strange, strange state of affairs to be wanting to go back to school. There's another reason too. My poems. I wonder what Mrs Goldstein thinks. She's probably forgotten them, or even thrown them away in disgust, thinking what a load of stupid pretentious angst-ridden adolescent bunk. She probably read them to her husband and had a good laugh. Oh, well. You've got to face up to the truth one day. At least I've had my name in the paper. No one can take that away.

We've got another heat wave. It's almost hotter than it was in Spain. We all ate supper outside last night, together. Mum and Dad snapped at each other about new garden furniture, i.e. Mum wanted to get one of those swing chairs with a canopy over it and Dad didn't. That just about sums up their relationship. I feel like things are going downhill on that front, somehow. I even found myself thinking that perhaps I'd better do something terrible again, maybe hitchhike to London or stay out all night. It's pretty weird, Alexa, to think I was considering taking up juvenile delinquency just to get them talking.

Would you believe it! Yesterday I arrived at the Fresh Bake at three o'clock and Sarry DIDN'T RECOGNIZE ME. She really didn't. She was sitting in our favourite window seat eating a Double Cream Special and when I said 'Hello' she looked up and said 'Oh, hi,' and then looked straight down again. Then she looked up and said, 'Jeez! *Gilly*. It's you.'

''course it's me,' I said.

'You've *grown*!' she said, staring at me with her mouth open. 'And you're getting boobs!' She was almost screeching. 'Shhh!' I said. I didn't want the whole clientele and staff of the Fresh Bake staring at my chest as if they expected to see the Great Trowton Bosom Miracle take place before their very eyes. 'Sh, sh!' I said.

And I told Sarry about my holiday and how I'd made it up with Annie. And Sarry told me about her holiday in Cornwall and said that she hoped we'd still be friends and I said not to be so daft and stuff like that. And we drooled over the cutting from the *Echo* for about half an hour, reading our names out loud and laughing about how Pennings must be ruing the day he sneered up his sleeve at us. Then I asked, casually, if she'd seen Judy and she said she hadn't but that she'd seen HIM *alone* at Tricks and wasn't that interesting. And it was!

I'm getting my dress for the wedding next Saturday. I spent all the last week trying to persuade Mum to give me the dosh so I could choose it for myself and went on and on about being nearly grown-up and all of my friends, etc., etc. But she just said she was sick and tired of that old record and she didn't want me turning up at the wedding looking like something that the cat had dragged in. For heaven's sake!

Rosalee's being really funny to me for some reason. She's probably furious that my bosoms are here. I expect she wishes that I'd got some mutant gene that would keep me forever locked in puppy-flabbed adolescence while she grows longer and more graceful every day. I expect that's what's getting her down. But I hardly deserve to be hated and ridiculed just because I've got hormones, like every other person that walks the earth. Do I?

Love

Gilly

23 *Tudor Avenue*
Benbridge
Trowton TR0 9AF

Ms Alexa Deerheart   1 September
THE BIZZ

Dear Alexa

It's beyond anything! I was feeling OK. All right. Until yesterday. I locked myself in the bathroom and didn't come out for THREE HOURS. And three hours sitting in a bathroom looking at Oriental Gardens wallpaper is pretty boring. I can tell you. But I was so angry, so fierce and raging furious that I would have stayed there all night if I could. Rosalee has *read my poems*! My new ones. She sneaked into my room and looked through all my things, including your letters. And, of course, she found the sock. She's ruined everything with her nasty mean embezzling of my private life. I feel like she's stolen my secrets because I haven't got them any more. I haven't, have I? She's just taken them and killed them with contempt and her horrible sneering.

I went to Annie's for tea yesterday. And, of course, it was great to be together again, but I've forgotten all that now. I got home about half-past eight and went straight to the bathroom for a nostril examination. The house was dead quiet. Dad was downstairs asleep in front of the telly, Mum was out and I thought Rosalee was out too until I heard this sniggering laugh coming from her room. So I went in to see what was so funny. What did I find? Rosalee with *all my stuff* on her lap, reading it.

'Oh, quite the little poet, aren't we?' she said. 'This is *really* good stuff.' And she started reading it out! I flew at her. I felt that murder, strangulation and pounding to a frazzle were probably the least I was capable of. But she jumped on her bed and held them up, snorting and saying, 'I suppose you think you're a genius, big brain. And who's this VISION, this lover boy of yours with "dark curling silken coils"? Sounds like a *snake*! And, oh God, listen to this. . . .'

I can understand crimes of passion, Alexa. I *pulled* Rosalee off the bed and started *pounding* into her. But she was stronger than me. She got on top of me and pinned my arms to the floor saying horrible, horrible things, like 'God, look at you, sweaty little creep, just because you've got little pimply tits you think you're God's gift. Hasn't anyone ever told you that you're ugly and fat, creep, eh? Do you seriously think anyone'd fancy *you*! And all this *garbage* poetry. It's rubbish.' I got a great *rush* of anger which shot through my bones giving me super-human strength. I *threw* her off me and kicked her, trying to rip my poems out of her hand at the same time, which tore them in two. 'Shut

200

up! Shut up!' I screamed, going for the throat, but I missed. She grabbed her pot of Biogenetic Primrose Cream and threw it at me. 'Bitch!' I yelled and ran into the bathroom just as Dad was coming up the stairs saying, 'For heaven's sake, what on earth is going on up here? World War Three?'

And I decided that I wasn't going to speak, ever again, to anyone. Dad was banging on the bathroom door and Rosalee was sitting in her bedroom pretending nothing had happened. It wasn't until Mum came home and told everybody to go downstairs that the sordid story was revealed.

'I'm *never* coming out,' I said. 'At least not until she gets down on her knees and apologizes.'

'Rosie, come up here at once,' said Mum, really crossly.

'She shouldn't touch my *things*; my *private* things!' I screamed.

And I could hear Rosalee mumbling in her horrible sulky voice, 'She shouldn't leave her stuff about, I only saw it by accident because I was looking for something in her wardrobe. And I don't see why I should apologize to *her*.' Lies, lies, Alexa. And on and on we went, round and round in circles until she finally said, 'OK. If I have to. *Sorry*,' which sounded more like Rosalee-speak for 'I hate your guts, creep.'

'She doesn't *mean it*,' I said. Really, what's

201

the point of someone apologizing if they don't mean it? It's even worse than a straightforward kick in the teeth. So in the end Rosalee had to agree to *give* me her pink Spandex, which was the only thing I would accept as a token of her absolute sincerity. So, I came out, tore into her room and yanked the Spandex from her drawer, but really it might as well have been a rotten old dishrag for all I cared. It was no substitute for the whole refuge of my secret life being stolen and screwed up and ruined and thrown away just to gratify Spite. As I said before, I sometimes think Rosalee is jealous of me, but she might as well be jealous of a fruit fly for all I've got left in the world now.

Do other people have sadistic mind torturers, calculating confidence killers, for sisters, eh? Or have I been cursed for some unforgivable crime of childhood that I've committed without knowing it?

Yours in total humiliation

Gilly

23 *Tudor Avenue*
Benbridge
Trowton TR0 9AF

Ms Alexa Deerheart   6 September
THE BIZZ

Dear Alexa

I just don't see how you can say that it's difficult for older sisters! It's not difficult for them *at all*. They get everything; they get to do everything first. Like walk and talk and go to school and get breasts and have boyfriends. It's us second comers who get the raw deal, forever behind being told 'she's the eldest' every five minutes and always having someone three steps ahead of you and *never* being able to catch up. That's what it's like.

Well, back at school, in a new year. We're 10a now, all except for Phyllis who's been kept down in Year Nine. Poor Phyllis. For years nobody takes a blind bit of notice of her floundering away in idiotic ignorance at the back of the class, no one bothers to give her extra lessons or tries to find out what's inside her. Then as soon as we start getting into the serious GCSE stuff, down she goes, dropped from the clouds like a stuffed tomato. Splat! I only hope the new 9a will treat her kindly. After all, it's not her fault, is it?

It was great to be sitting next to Annie again. There was a dodgy moment when Annie, Em, Sarry and me were all standing round and Tracey came up and said, 'Who're you sitting next to, Annie?' just like that, straight out. And Annie said she was sitting next to me in class, but would sit next to her in English, if she wanted. And Brainbox made this funny sort of nasal whine as if to say, I don't care, please yourself. And I thought, Well, what does she expect. Annie and I have been best friends for *eight* years, and you can't replace that just because you can do multiple fractions in your head and recite the complete works of William Shakespeare off by heart. I mean, what use are those things in a crisis, eh?

But even though everyone was really nice (Annie said she thought I'd grown and Em said my tan made my eyes stand out and they all noticed my bumps) I still felt downright dejected, low, beaten down by Rosalee's rotten attack on my inner life which had succeeded in regressing me back to the nothing-lump of former days. I just couldn't pull myself out of it. And, of course, all the time I was agonizing about whether Mrs Goldstein had read my poems and what she thought and whether she would say anything, especially now Rosalee had already judged them unfit for anything but a good long sneering laugh.

And I was so wrapped up in my inner soul musings that it wasn't until morning break that

I noticed Judy wasn't there! Nobody knew where she was.

Then at lunchtime Kelly Stewart, who lives next door but one to Judy, stunned us with the revelation that Judy has come out in a hideous scarlet rash *all over her body*. Apparently she is lying in bed with a sheet over her refusing to see anybody. And it was, said Kelly, all a nervous reaction to the fact that HE had ditched her after the holiday and she couldn't face coming back to school. What do you think of *that*! But HE was there, glorious one. Even longer and leaner and as smooth and brown as toffee. A feast for the eye; food for the soul. A banquet for the senses. I wonder if he's noticed my bumps, or even noticed me at all. I doubt it.

We spent most of the morning drawing up our new timetables, but I couldn't concentrate. I was in a sort of anxiety phase about everything and kept drifting off into other worlds. There was my desert-island-love-paradise world, there was my revenge-on-Rosalee-Freeborn world, and the will-Mrs-Goldstein-remember-my-poems world which was foremost in my mind when the bell rang for lunch. I looked down at my paper. I'd written, 'Wed. 3 p.m. Mrs Gupta. Cookery and domestic lovesock.'

Well, Alexa, I was feeling rotten by the time we got to English lit. Mrs Goldstein was very brown and looked about ten years younger than she did before the holidays. She was quite funny actually, telling us about her trip to Italy and how at dinner she called out 'calamari' instead of 'cameriere' which means waiter, and they slapped this huge great slithery octopus with all its legs on in front of her, its eyes staring up from the plate. And she had to *eat* it because it was the chef's speciality. Ugh!

We didn't do any real work. She just talked about how hard we *would* be working this term and how important all this *hard work* was going to prove in our future careers as brain surgeons and prime ministers, and how we might not realize it now but we would be thankful in years to come and all the usual stuff that grown-ups go on and on about ad infinitum and for ever. Then suddenly it was half-past three. She didn't even look at me. Everyone was grabbing their things and tearing out. *She's not going to say anything* I was thinking. She's forgotten, or she's too embarrassed because my poems are so awful she can't bring herself to mention them in case she bursts into hysterical laughter. And then she was packing up her bag to go. Well, that's it, I thought. Rosalee was right.

So I picked up all my stuff and was just following Annie out of the door when she said, 'Oh, Gillian. I'd forgotten I wanted to speak to you. Stay behind for a minute, please.'

I stood there going red in the face and feeling stupid for even thinking that my dreadful outpourings were worth someone giving up time to look at them when they could be doing something a million times more interesting like washing up or cleaning out their ears.

'Well,' said Mrs Goldstein, taking my blue book out of her bag. 'You're quite a surprise, aren't you? First the essay and now these.'

'Umph,' I said, looking down and examining the pattern in the sludge-grey floor tiles.

'I think some of these are very good,' she said. 'You've got some lovely ideas. They really made me smile.'

'Umph,' I said. 'But they're not really meant to be funny, Miss.'

'I know,' said Mrs Goldstein, smiling. 'What I mean is that you've got an *original* way of looking at the world, that's very, well, interesting.'

'Do you really mean it?' I said. 'You're not just saying it?'

'You know me better than that,' said Mrs Goldstein. 'There's some splendid rhythm in some of these verses. The words sing.'

Alexa, that's what she said. She said the words sing. And I told her what Rosalee had said and she said that older sisters couldn't always be expected to appreciate their younger siblings' talents, and I'd have to understand that. And I asked her not to tell anyone about the poems because they were my own secret and I wasn't ready yet to launch myself on the world. And she said OK, but she'd be expecting a lot from me this term. And I said, OK.

Alexa, I'm keeping all this to myself. Secrets are precious things, aren't they? This truth I found out at very painful cost. But I've got some of them back now, to keep inside where Rosalee can't get her sweaty mitts on them.

I've got my new dress for Saturday. It's silvery blue with a short, swingy skirt. I'm going to write a poem for Auntie Paula's wedding, wishing her luck.

Love

Gilly Freeborn (poet)

To Paula

> *Your sculptured candles shone*
> *For Tom*
> *But he couldn't see*
> *Your special light,*
> *Your golden flame.*
> *So now you're going to wed*
> *Fred.*

23 Tudor Avenue
Benbridge
Trowton TR0 9AF

Ms Alexa Deerheart   10 September
THE BIZZ

Dear Alexa

I feel sad. I don't know why, but I've got a feeling this may be the last letter I'll write to you, somehow. I expect you're all agog to hear about the wedding and Mum and Dad and stuff and how things are going on all fronts. There's so much to tell.

Well, it's Sunday now. We all got up really early yesterday to prepare for the big day. Rosalee was trying to make it up, being sort of *helpful*, trying to pull the older sister advice thing. I suppose that it's pretty difficult to carry around a great weight of *guilt* and *lies* and still have people smile at you as if you were a nice, normal human person who has a right to walk the earth. I suppose that's pretty hard. I hadn't spoken to her since the bathroom episode. I hadn't even *looked* at her, not straight in the eye. I had stayed in my room, trying to stick my broken poems together with Sellotape – a tragic picture of a sensitive young life ruined. So the grievous consequences of her actions finally must have filtered through because on

209

Friday she started *smiling* at me and on Saturday she bounded into my room first thing saying, 'Hey, Gilly, do you want me to do your make-up? I've got some lovely glittery blue eye shadow that will go with your dress.' Oh, pitiful, shallow girl!

'I'm sorry,' I replied with dignity. 'I can't talk to you. I don't want you even near me, I might get contaminated.'

I sat in the garden till eleven, topping up my tan. Mum and Dad were arguing again, their screaming and screeching flying out of the window to invade the ears of our neighbours like some kitchen-sink radio play. Dad was saying he was wearing his old white linen suit and his tartan bow tie and that was that. And Mum was saying that she didn't want her family to be a laughing stock and she'd had his silver mohair cleaned specially, and on and on and on. So by the time we got down to some serious getting ready, everyone was in a thoroughly bad mood.

I suppose you'll think I'm a real hypocrite, Alexa, but Rosalee did end up doing my make-up. You see, I'd forgotten about shoes. My red shoes with the heels were all scuffed, and that only left my flat brown sandals and my Dr Martens. Nothing went with my blue dress. We had a big panic and in the end Rosalee said I could borrow her black patent high heeled mules. She just offered them saying, 'They'll look really nice, Gilly.' I knew they were her favourites, her pride and joy, so I started to forgive her then, just a bit. I sat on her bed to try them on and she said, 'It'll only take me five minutes to do your face. Go on, Gill, sit down.'

So I did. I sat at Rosalee's dressing table while she flicked and brushed and stroked and patted and rubbed and plucked. It was strange looking at this new brown face, my face, gradually changing. It wasn't like me, or how I thought I was. It wasn't bad, I suppose.

I was ready first. I put on my blue dress and the patent mules; the dress was all scratchy against my bumps but I didn't mind – at least it proved they were still there. I brushed my hair back off my face, took a deep breath and looked at myself in the full-length mirror. At that precise moment Dad came in looking for a hairbrush and said, 'Heavens, Gillykins, is that you!' in astonished tones. And all I will say, Alexa, is that I was pretty astonished myself. For the first time in my life I didn't look like a stumpy-legged *blob*. In fact, my legs actually looked quite *long*.

Quarter to one and Mum was still in her bedroom. It looked as if her whole wardrobe was scattered over the bed. She was in such a panic she didn't even look at me. 'Oh, hell, Gilly,' she said. 'I don't like my new suit, the skirt's too frumpy. It makes me look middle-aged. What'n earth am I going to wear?'

I knew. Buried at the back of her wardrobe

was this lovely floaty dress like lots of scarves sewn together. It had little shoulder straps and a low back. I took it out. 'Wear this one,' I said.

'Oh, for heaven's sake!' said Mum laughing. 'That's ancient. I haven't worn it for years. Anyway, it's too young for me now.'

'No it's not,' I said. 'It's lovely. Try it on.'

'All right, just for a laugh,' she said. 'Bet I can't even get into it.'

But she could, Alexa. She looked absolutely beautiful. And she ummed and ahhhed and ummed and ahhhed, but she could see she looked beautiful too, and when Rosalee came in and said, 'Wow!' that was it.

The wedding was all over in about two minutes. Auntie Paula was wearing *black cycling shorts* and a big blousy shirt with penguins on it. The mysterious Fred was wearing a T-shirt and sort of balloon trousers that looked like they'd been made from a parachute. Bit odd for a wedding, I was thinking. Mum said, 'Typical! She's as daft as your dad,' under her breath, but she was smiling all the same. Afterwards we rushed out and hurled confetti at them. But Auntie Paula said she didn't need it, whatever that meant.

We all drove off to this big house in the country for the reception. It was a lovely warm evening, the kind you only get in September when the colours are all glowing and it's sort of breezy. Auntie Paula and Fred stood in the doorway giving everyone a glass of champagne, even me! Paula shrieked when she saw me and said, 'Gilly, I hardly know you!' which I think was a compliment. There was a huge buffet, vegetarian of course, in a great big ballroom type place with tables all around the dance floor. Each table had one of Paula's sculptured candles on it. We had a sort of elongated mushroom on ours which Dad seemed to find hilarious for some reason.

Then, Alexa, Mum took off her jacket. Dad was staring, stark staring with his eyes nearly popping out of his head. She looked so lovely, all thin and floaty in the scarf-dress. He looked sort of *mesmerized*, as if he'd had an electric shock or something. 'Fetch me a glass of wine, will you please, Gilly,' said Mum coolly. Then she flicked her hair and gave Dad a very funny look as if to say, *See*.

Rosie and I went off to the bar, Rosie striding ahead, wriggling her red-spotted bottom in a flaunty way. I was a bit tottery on my high heels, but I was getting used to them. I could actually walk quite well if I took small steps. Then, Alexa, the most extraordinary thing happened. The most astonishing thing in the history of astonishing things. I thought I was going mad; stark staring raving mad, mind-damaged. I thought perhaps my hormones had done something to my brain and sent me over the edge. My fantasies were taking me over, materializing in front of my eyes like ectoplasm. But there, leaning on the bar, wearing a black open-neck shirt and grey chinos and drinking a glass of beer was HIM! HE. THE ONE. I stood stock-still, frozen rigid. I blinked and blinked again, but it wasn't until Rosalee said, 'God, who's *that*!' that I believed he was really there. Jonathan O'Neil was at Auntie Paula's wedding. *My* Auntie Paula's wedding. Standing there within my gaze, alone. And I felt sick. I felt sick because Rosalee had suddenly come to vivid life and was *flicking her hair* and *pursing her lips* and smoothing her red spots over her hips and going all jaunty and shiny. Rosalee, with her long legs and browny blonde hair. He would probably fall in love with her *on the spot*.

'Oh, look! There's Jonathan,' came enthusiastic tones from behind. It was Auntie Paula. 'You *know* him?' said Rosalee all agog. 'Of course,' said Auntie Paula. 'He's Fred's nephew. A bit of a dish, isn't he? Come on, I'll introduce you.' Before I had time to absorb 'Fred's nephew' into my brain cells Auntie Paula grabbed our arms and propelled us towards him at lightning speed.

I can't recall exactly what happened next, Alexa. I have this hazy memory of gibbering inanities like 'what a coincidence' and 'fancy that' and Rosalee pushing in front of me, elbowing me in the ribs saying, 'You'd better

get the wine, Gilly. Mum 'n' Dad are waiting.'
So I left them. Sloped off. Heart-sick. Who
said all's fair in Love? Nothing's fair, not even
Chance.

Dad was still staring blankly at Mum when
I got back with their drinks. I flopped back in
my seat and sipped my champagne, letting the
bubbles fizz in my nose. The party was starting
to liven up, people were dancing and laughing
and having fun. I was thinking, I just can't
believe this, I just can't take it in. It was as if this
dream-like opportunity had been deliberately
thrown at me just to be snatched back again.
It was as if Fate was singing 'Na-na-na-na-na,
the Gods are not with you, Gilly Freeborn.
Love's fortunes are not for the likes of you.
And it's about time you faced up to it.' I half
expected Phyllis Bean to rise up from the floor,
carrot cake oozing from her mouth, crying
Gilly! *Gilly*!

Mum and Dad still hadn't spoken. They
were sitting there like shop-window dummies.
I got really fed up with them, especially Dad,
always whingeing on and moaning about the
world letting him down. I was thinking he was
bloody lucky to have someone as lovely as
Mum and that you can't expect people to stay
the same for ever. And he did look daft, Alexa,
in that tartan bow tie.

I wandered off and stood in a dark corner
to watch the dancing. After about ten minutes
HE emerged from the bar with Rosalee sold-

ered to his side, attacking him with her sex vibes. It was impossible to tell if he was responding, but I hardly cared. I felt so furious and jealous, Alexa, it was like nothing on earth. For a moment it looked as if they were coming towards me. I couldn't bear it, I *glowered* at them through my fringe, threw them a lethal glance as if to say, Don't you dare come near me. I don't want you flaunting love's young dream in my face.

I slunk away and found Auntie Paula who gave me another glass of champagne saying she knew she shouldn't but I looked like I needed cheering up, which was the understatement of the century. Then she said I was looking very grown-up and that Rosalee would have to watch out soon. Soon is too late, I thought. But Auntie Paula was all funny and silly and she cheered me up. It's a talent she's got.

We both found ourselves staring at Mum and Dad, sitting there frozen in stalemate, neither of them willing to make the first move. 'Your mum looks gorgeous tonight,' said Auntie Paula. 'I do wish they'd sort themselves out. God, I remember when Gordon first met your mum, you'd have thought there was no other woman on earth. He drove us all mad.' Suddenly, I had a brainwave, Alexa. 'What was Dad's favourite song, Auntie Paula?' I said. 'When he was young.'

'God,' she said. 'Well, he loved John Lennon. Especially "Imagine".'

'Will you ask if they've got it?' I said. 'And if they have, get them to play it really loud.'

Half an hour later it came drifting out of the speakers and over to our table where it landed smack in the middle of Mum and Dad. Something happened, because for the first time in recent memory they actually *looked at each other*, straight in the eyes. Dad even looked quite tearful for a moment. It was getting through. 'Come on, you old bag,' he said suddenly and dragged Mum on to the dance floor.

I don't know if it'll last, Alexa. But I left them there, actually dancing, holding each other, while

> *You may say I'm a dreamer*
> *But I'm not the only one*

did its stuff.

I wandered outside and sat on the steps, feeling fed up and left out. Then I started thinking and dreaming, listening to the wind and the far-off noises of the world churning round. Come on, I thought. You've got to start your own life, you've got to stop worrying about all these *other* things that you can't control. You're *not* a nothing person, really. The wind was cold, making goosepimples on my arms, but I didn't care. I suddenly got this great welling up in my chest, like joy.

I must have been sitting there for ages, when I felt a rush of air as the door opened.

217

Something brushed against my neck, soft and tingly. A voice, barely audible, said, 'Wanna dance, you funny girl?' He grabbed my arm and we walked up the steps, I put my head on his shoulder. Some things you don't forget, like songs. The French Sisters were singing, '*Time goes on, we move we change/Our hearts are drifting on the ebb and flow of time. . . .*'

My bumps rubbed against his chest. I didn't faint or wobble. I felt my eyes grow wide and clear. I felt some sort of power shoot through my arms to my fingertips. I felt I could lift up the world. I thought, Whatever happens, I don't mind. I can win a prize. I can make words sing. Emily would have understood.

Love, Alexa, and thanks

Gillian Freeborn